DECODING THE PHOENIX

MD Tchaves

This is a fictionalized account of a true event. Any resemblance to actual persons, living or dead, is purely coincidental.

Publisher: Shoot for the Stars Publishing—Great Neck, NY
ISBN: 978-0-692-92282-8
Card Catalogue Number: 2017949660
Title: *Decoding the Phoenix* | MD Tchaves
Available Formats:
eBook distribution | Shoot for the Stars Publishing
Paperback | Shoot for the Stars Publishing, 2017

DEDICATION

This book is dedicated to the following people who keep me intellectually honest and always have me striving to expand my thought streams. I hope this book makes its way to you one day.

Joe Rogan, Kevin Smith, Jesse Ventura, Jordan Maxwell, Santos Bonacci, Bashar, Russell Brand, Robert David Steele, Karen Hudes, Dan Brown Victor Zammitt and David Wilcock.

I'd also like to thank my fiancé and soon to be wife Antonia for supporting me and standing by me while I wrote this.

"You can't convince a believer of anything; for their belief is not based on evidence, it's based on a deep seated need to believe."
—Carl Sagan

CHAPTER 1

I can't believe I'm about to do this. They're not going to let what I'm about to do slide, and they're definitely going to figure out how to kill me for it. You think I'm dramatic, don't you? But, see, I'm not. Before I get too far ahead of myself and, what's infinitely worse, you, let me start over. My name is Graham Newsdon and I know the answer to the world's deepest secret. The question that you've always wanted answered. The one Pascal, da Vinci, Einstein, Newton, and Hawking all struggled with. I know the truth and have peace because of it, even though it almost cost me my life—and still might. What I mean is that I am going to share my story with you and, for that, they will come after me.

If you'd tied me down to a chair two years ago and forced me into a meeting with the me talking right now and made him listen to the information I am going to share with you, he would have called me crazy, even if he had recognized his own reflection talking to him. There is an ancient saying, probably from Egypt, that goes, "You can lead a camel to water, but you can't make him drink." There's another equally poignant one: "If a man is thirsty, pour him some water out of your jar, but fill his glass up halfway. If he is still thirsty he will ask for more, if not, then he is satisfied or perhaps wasn't thirsty to begin with." Think about that for a few, while you decide if you want to hear my story.

There you go, thinking it again: this guy is a wackaloon. A brilliant comedian once said, "The worst thing to call somebody is crazy. It's dismissive. 'I don't understand this person. So they're crazy.' That's bullshit. These people are not crazy. They're strong people. Maybe their environment is a little sick."

So, can I talk to you in metaphors all day? If it gets the point across, of course, but you'd probably rip your hair out. Allow it for a few moments because it's important that I lay some groundwork here. If I just started hemorrhaging information, you would be freaked out. Truth be told, it took me almost a year to fully grasp all these functioning metaphors in relation to presenting knowledge to people and to understand group and individual dynamics, inflection, tone, people's biases, and their need to hold onto indoctrination. Understanding the psychopathology of myself from an outside perspective has helped me understand how to approach other individuals. The top of Graham's pyramid is Refuting the Central Point, which occurs when you do just that. The bottom is Name-Calling and right above it is the Ad Hominem attack, which involves calling people conspiracy theorists or crazy. This does not actually address the information presented; instead, it panders to a person's biases. Point blank and simple, it is low-brow intelligence collusion of opinion-molding. We all fall in different areas up and down this pyramid; the idea is to be cognizant of where we are at all times. I come from a Fulbright family and was going to Harvard Medical School when my life unraveled. Here's hoping you are smarter than me and can catch on faster because our lives and the future of the planet's civilization depends on you accepting what I have to share with you.

CHAPTER 2

(SEVEN MONTHS AGO)

I missed the call. Or multiple calls, I should say. One minute I'm learning about bedside manner and the current HIPAA guidelines and the next I'm walking through the famed lavender fields in France near where my mother grew up. In the distance, I see the house that I was raised in and I try to walk toward it, but my legs won't work and I collapse. I start to crawl and as I do, the fields dry up and the color fades. I reach out for the house but it is no use—my legs are concrete blocks. Suddenly I hear a loud popping noise and I am jolted awake to Hannah making a contorted face at me like she forgot how to read. This is not the first time she's jolted me out of deep REM sleep.

"You really should quit school and sell roses by the freeway exit. I'll love you no matter what you do, but this is killing you. Our kids are going to be holiday-wrapping Ambien for you. Did Blur keep you up late last night again?" Hannah said lovingly, or as lovingly as someone who says that kind of thing can pass off.

What makes people want to reproduce before

they're financially ready? Or at least talk about it? I don't know why this pissed me off so much but it did. I get it. Maybe two-hundred years ago when your lifespan was fifty years and you didn't have student loans because you were a coal miner, to have babies at twenty-three fell halfway through your life. Or five- to six-hundred years ago, to get your groove on earlier because your lifespan was thirty-five or forty years. For all the romantics out there, Romeo and Juliet were nineteen and thirteen respectively; just remember that. Today that gets you a one-way ticket to pound-me-in-the-ass prison. What really gets to me is my old girlfriends from the crew back in Georgetown undergrad with kids who like to complain to me about sleep. Try medical school. Sleep? Really?

Sorry, we were in the middle of introductions, right? Hannah Dean Husker. Love of my life. Father died in a car accident a month before she was born, so her mother gave her his name to carry on. Dean, by the way; not Hannah. In case you were confused, insert head in toilet and flush. We share the same birthday and every March 21 I like to remind her that she was born an hour before me. They say women outlive men by five years on average and it's this great mystery to scientists. Is it the physical labor? Is it genetics? Negative—it's self-defense, the ultimate passive aggressiveness. Scientists still can't figure out why people sometimes just spontaneously combust. The M.E. at the morgue should test the dearly departed for girlfriends, mistresses, and wives. I'm still waiting for the Nobel committee to call. So Blur is this underground alternative news source that my best friend Nerds Pierce or, as I call him, NP, is certifiably obsessed with. Why Nerds? Children are creative, aren't they? When growing up your best friend has been in MENSA since he was eleven, what can you really do? I honestly wish there was a more creative story for you. I don't get what the big deal is with this guy. Personally, I've got better things to do than entertain insane theories of the world and government. Life can't be as psychotic as this guy babbles on about. When Blur gets his loud pastor sermon going and NP's pupils grow wide like he just sat on a PEZ dispenser filled with ecstasy, I feel like locking him and the TV in a sauna together and bringing over one of those witch doctors with a bone through his nose to detox the living room.

Then there's Jean, my roommate since undergrad at Georgetown; he thinks NP is certifiable. He comes from the wealthy Solex oil family overseas and is in Harvard Business School as one of your obligatory rich with a life forced upon him. Lucky for him, he somehow escaped pubescence with a personality and sense of humor to combat the douchebaggery of his predisposition. He'd kill me if he knew I mentioned this, but he loves foreign women and I can't think of a better place besides gift-carding him money to a mail-order bride website for him to flex his talents than Harvard, let alone the business school. Also, if it weren't for his generosity, I'd likely be up to my kneecaps in filet mignon cat food and scurvy for the remainder of med school. He knows how I only eat organic food and keep the house filled with things that the normal person would consider fertilizer. Basically, if karma exists, I have to be his serf in the afterlife.

Back to NP. I can't bring myself to be too hard on this walking Ritalin clinical trial and his vast knowledge of everything you could think of. He is an encyclopedia of the most outrageous things you could imagine. I'm getting all warm and fuzzy just thinking about you meeting him. We ended up at the same high school for gifted kids, Clever Interlock High. I guess the powers that name schools figured the students were intelligent and should have their minds molded toward the future together. We also both got accepted to Georgetown University, but at the last minute he decided against it. He was picked up by this startup that seems to be taking off in the general Mass area called The Zip Code Bandits. He writes a few articles a week about what's going on in his town. A bunch of other people who work for this company have other areas they do the same for and once or twice a week they meet together and compare notes and give one another ideas. Basically the idea is that this will spread like a virus. Eventually all you will need to do is login to this website, type in your zip code, and get real-time news about what's going on in your area, no crap from the media, as he puts it. He's written a few articles recently like "What Is *Really* in Your Water Supply?" and "Don't Eat Me! I'll Destroy Your Insides." Kid has a gift for writing, in a very spastic colon sort of way. The last article isn't what you think, although I shouldn't explain it to you because it'll be more fitting to let you picture him this way. He discusses a phone app for people who are too lazy to do research into what's actually in their food. You point and click with your phone once the app is downloaded and it tells you if something is healthy or not. If not, basically how it will kill you. Perfect for busy soccer moms who actually care about their children but don't have a year's worth of free time to research. This last one he wrote up absolutely slays me. He tries this thing on cherry and strawberry yogurt, not the fruit at the bottom kind. A giant skull and bones comes up. You click on the picture and a warning sign flashes like when that Japanese power plant was about to blow and everyone ignored it. (I guess this inventor has a thing for theatrics.) It has carmine, gelatin, aspartame, and castoreum. Carmine is what gives dark red food color its, well, color. They get it by extracting the carminic acid from drying beetles and then boiling them to extract the color. Gelatin is mostly the collagen, which is taken from animal bones. Anybody who has enjoyed Jell-O has already enjoyed this. Aspartame is your sugar-free Equal; it's what makes diet soda diet and it's what makes these yogurts low-fat or no-fat. It's produced by genetically modified E. coli, force-feeding it fossil fuels, then cultivating the waste byproduct. No, you read that sentence right. Apparently aspartame poisoning mimics Parkinson's and many doctors prescribe Parkinson's medicine for aspartame poisoning, and these people never get better. Lastly, castoreum is what is used to make strawberry or raspberry or vanilla artificial flavoring. It's also used in expensive perfumes. It is a yellowish secretion of the castor sac, which is located between the crotch and the anus of the North American beaver. Again, you read that sentence correctly. Internal beaver juice is being used to flavor your yogurts and thanks to their expensive perfumes, women are spraying themselves with it. Anyway, that's NP and he loves it. He's there right now at work trying to save the world. Actually, take that back; no, he's not. He's in my doorway out of breath, looking at me like I put Visine in his apple juice.

"What's the point of owning a cell phone if you don't pick it up?"

"I'll dump it when I get the first chance," I retorted, trying to sound as obnoxious as possible.

"Well, have you spoken to Rose yet," he said as he came in and started to rustle around my cluttered table for my cell phone.

Damn. I knew I'd forgotten someone. Rosette Rebel. Best girl friend since in utero. We all came from a rather large utero, just in case you're worried about us suffering from Crush Syndrome. Also, she is NP's obsession since I can remember. Think Urkel if Viagra was around in the eighties. Make that Screech and Lisa. Growing up ten minutes outside of Boston, all of us had pretty awesome childhoods. We always had the coolest new snacks and toys. Only while everyone's parents let their kids play shooting games, Rose and NP would come over to play videogame versions of *Jeopardy*, *Wheel of Fortune*, *Family Feud*, and *Pictionary*. Hmm, I guess that actually explains a lot.

"Did you hear me?" he said.

"Sorry, I was thinking. Yeah, hold on. Quit messing around my desk. I'll check my voicemail," I said, trying hard not to be annoyed about his cluttering of my already cluttered desk. I mean, it's already messy, but at least I know where everything is. I tried to let that go as I checked my messages.

"Newsdon, your mom's been trying to reach you; where the crap are you? Call her right away." Rose hung up abruptly, halfway through her last word. She's one of those. I didn't like her tone. Ever get that feeling when your heart starts beating in your throat? I dialed my mother.

"Mom, hi," I said anxiously.

"No, drunk. Very drunk," she said, snapping me immediately into hyper focus mode. "There has been an accident."

"What kind of accident?" I shouted into the phone. I'm not one for dancing around the flowers on things; if you have information, the sooner you can force your lips to vomit the words the better.

"I'm sorry, sweetie," she continued. "Your brother has left us."

At this point, I remember very little. The phone sliding out of my hand, the corners of my vision turning slightly off, like a bad movie projector or like I stared into the sun too long and was seeing spots. Jean, who was in the other room waiting on a phone call for a job interview, saw me stumble and ran out and picked up the phone and finished the conversation with my mother.

"Je suis vraiment desole mon ami. There's no way to make this any easier, so let's get the information out and then deal with it, okay? They are calling it a suicide. His platoon just got back from a mission that was top-secret. Apparently they can't tell you where he was or what he was doing, but they are bringing his platoon home and giving them all medals and they would like you to go to DC to accept his posthumously. Veux tu que je viennes avec toi to our old stomping grounds," Jean suggested, while trying to be as simpatico as possible regarding the situation.

The next five hours were a bit blurry for me on account of that bottle of Absinthe I'd snuck back through customs on Hannah's and my vacation to Europe. Rosette showed up eventually and thankfully stopped NP from pouring out statistics about PTSD and military suicide. One thing was for sure, though. Well, two things. Absinthe always needs to be watered and sugared down—you could run your generator off it—and there was no way I was not going. I needed answers.

CHAPTER 3

I hate flying. If I didn't have family overseas, I'd never board a plane. At home, if I can help it, I take an Amtrak. I was also hung-over and in no condition to drive. Two days of trying to numb the pain didn't really do much except make me feel worse. Fortunately, I whittled a go-go gadget saline IV with a coat hanger hooked to the coat rack overhead and threaded my own vein. Also, NP gifted me a CamelBak worth of Pedialyte. According to him, things like iced tea and sodas are caffeinated, which actually do the opposite of hydrating you. This is why you should never drink iced tea when you're thirsty. Also, I knew this but I was too hungover to remind him that I was in medical school and knew what electrolytes are. Luckily, Jean and I were exhausted and slept through much of the trip. Isn't it funny how you cannot relate to time when you are asleep? Six hours of sleep feels like twenty minutes, yet REM sleep that's only twenty-seconds long can feel like a three-hour dream. I guess we all experience the bending of space and time in that way. This full sleep was probably the longest I have slept since middle school. Then, why I was awakened hit me like a ton of bricks. The IV was apparently gone and I felt like I was storing enough pee to flood the train. So I made my way to the car with the bathroom.

As I was unloading that which my kidneys had filtered, I started to think straight for the first time in a few days. It dawned on me that I had an e-mail James had sent me that I hadn't yet opened. Unfortunately, I didn't bring my tablet with me and I don't have a Smartphone. This would have to wait until we got to the SAB's.

Right. I forgot to mention that. It was going to be about two days to get these Marines back home from said random place. We would be staying with our old fraternity brothers at the house. I hadn't visited my Sigma Alpha Beta, aka Sons-a-Bitches, since I left ol' George's Town, and it was currently smack in the middle of a mess with pledges week. Well, isn't it always a mess with pledges week? Sorry. Let me rephrase: hell week. We pulled up a block away and paid the taxi off. Jean has this thing where he doesn't want the cabbie to know where we are going, ever. We pulled up to 223 Bouillon Square and it was just as I remembered it. So front and center this house, almost dancing in the middle of the street and taunting the rest of the houses like a crazed drunk. It's amazing how thin walls can still hide the craziest of truths from people. There is nothing but these two aged doors between the world and inside. If I were to leave the doors open and let strangers see what may be going on inside: Demerol shots for everyone and straightjackets after the police were called. Probably cuckoo's-nest sentencing, maybe hate-crime charges.

The frat has the same setup they always had when it comes to how to get inside the house. There's a bush outside and on this bush is this really old ascot sweater. Under the ascot is a key that hooks to the bush. People wouldn't think there is a key there because, well, it's an old dirty piece of clothing, very charming decor. The key opens the metal box that's chained to the rail next to the door and the bush. In the box, there are cards for different stages of membership in the fraternity. Pledge, brother, alumni, then some cards that supersede what is well above my pay grade. You pick your card up and slide it under the door. The slot opens in the door, in the middle, by your chest, and you reach your hand all the way in and do the handshake. I've heard rumors that if you get it wrong as a pledge, they handcuff it to bars on the inside. I've never had the pleasure. I've also heard that if it's a busy Friday night and a pledge really screws it up, a few of the brothers dress up like Friar Tuck, go around the back exit to the front with the motherboard, our sacred frat paddle, which is really a boat oar, and spank the pledge while chanting incantations. Explain that to passersby. I've heard these videos have gotten several-million views on the Internet.

Our timing is the stuff legends are made of. I must admit this took my mind off my brother for a minute and actually made me laugh because I forgot how totally ridiculous it was. One of the traditions we have is a birth ritual. Everyone wears white and silver and stands outside in a giant circle while the pledges, one by one, share their biggest goals in life while pretending to give birth. I mean, really get into the contractions and the birth pains. Some members take a paintbrush with red paint and throw it on them while others spray ketchup like a Jackson Pollock-seizured inspiration, all the while these pledges try and deliver this Cabbage Patch baby. This is supposed to symbolize their re- birth into society and the beginning of them realizing themselves as being all they can be and that they can lean on one another to help them get to that level. A sort of born-again ritual if you will, and please do not read into that. We stayed for a few minutes to watch; Jean even went and filled some water balloons with paint to drop on pledges from a ladder. Some people never change.

I didn't stick around for the second half because next they would be going outside to the courtyard in the dark screaming their biggest regrets in life, while trying to give CPR to and trying to revive a skeleton. Legend has it the skeleton is real and belongs to a student who worked for the paper about a hundred years ago and who tried unsuccessfully to break into our fraternity. Supposedly he figured out where we kept the key but was unsuccessful once he threw the card under the door because he didn't know the handshake. He was cuffed to the door, but started acting like a pregnant hyena and was let go to avoid a larger scene. He then made a huge scene about it on campus, which only led to further ridicule, as nobody took him seriously or even cared. As legend has it, he died of the Spanish Flu not long after, but who really knows. Some brothers a few years later, once the rumors settled down, located his grave and dug up his skeleton. This is the person these pledges will be engaging within the necro foreplay and it's supposed to symbolize that you must always consider every angle in your life because the slightest slip-up can cost you everything in the end. I lived this once; plus, I had an e-mail to read. My little's little set me up in his room while he went to merge herpes with this cadaver. Great way to spend $58,000 a year, right?

"Ça va? Are you sure you want to do this?" Jean asked honestly. It was amazing how he could turn off the antics from a few moments prior and snap into a serious conversation.

"The code to the fridge is still the birthday of

that dirty bones pile that would give Hitchcock an orgasm. Please grab a bottle of the organic vodka that's been there for years, since nobody but me touched it, and a bottle of OJ. Give me a few minutes, please," I said.

"Bien sur," he replied as he started to leave.

"Hey Jean," I began. "Thanks for tagging along. You're a true friend. I'm not sure this would have worked if Hannah had come instead."

"De rien, Graham. Besides, she's with you. I'm pretty sure kissing a disgusting bone isn't the end of the world for her." He laughed.

"Truly, you are the ultimate asshole-face," I replied calmly.

As I dropped my face and opened the e-mail, it had occurred to me that this e-mail had sat in my inbox for over six months. What must have happened was that he sent it when I was out partying and it slipped through the cracks between my hangovers. Also, I mean, I recognized it was from him, but it wasn't from his standard military e-mail address. What kept me from opening it? I didn't realize it at the time, but life has a way of cutting you small breaks that you don't immediately understand, but with the benefit of hindsight you realize could have seriously changed the course of your life.

From: Unknown To Graham NewsdonGNewsdon@Hydragua.com
Subject: Teddy Sent: Feb 2, 2020

Happy Groundhog Day, Teddy. Tell me, did the groundhog see his shadow? Ain't no groundhogs round where we are. If you turn around to look at your shadow, you're liable to get your ass cheeks blown clear off. Sorry to send you mail from the road, but sometimes you just have to talk to your little brother. Also, I was given a weekend off and pretty much spent all my money traveling and seeing what I could. I want to share so much with you!

There are just seven of us left here, Teddy. I hope to get out soon but I doubt it, brother. If I could do it all over, I would have been a bartender at a top-dollar strip club. I'd just have to walk back and forth with pitchers of Adam's Ale, that sweet ambrosia, all the while I get to watch the S&M show on stage. Am I the only one who finds it hard to be a crab while the retro beetles, the *original* beetle roster was comin' out that stereo treble during twin virgin night? That would be the Greatest Of All Time. Cupid has shot me with an arrow. Entertainers, politicians, businessmen drooling over these ladies, throwing their money around like nothing. I'd make a ton. Baby bro, I'm trying to tell you something, so listen up to the sky,

okay, and I mean the oral pun? So much blind anger can only be cured by learning. Don't be seduced by the mean and lying brand. You must keep a close eye on the nearby priests, those Presbyterians. These brainy pesters, rise spy banter inside the binary gland. Their mission is to inundate an army of nearby pets sir to release mostly on Easter and Halloween. Speaking of Halloween, actually, remember that Halloween when I dressed you up like a lion? I still carry that picture with me. It was hysterical. Remember that crazy ice storm out of nowhere that happened that day and how it tore up your costume? Remember before that happened how I buried you up to your head in the backyard sandbox. I show people the photo but it's stupid because you were facing the wrong way. Looking at that picture of the lion helps me keep my perspective in the right direction.

Sadly that's not how my life worked out. Sorry to give you those disturbing images but they discourage that kind of talk where I am. That banned army ling mmmmkay? Ironic since I'm living in warzone conditions. Being in med school, I'm sure you know all about sleep deprivation, lack of food, feeling like you're up to your neck in water all the time. A nerve jets us constantly. I'm almost out, but with the secret stop-loss program and quiet wars being fought, who knows. This fight we're in, it's really the ankh reused, everyone

needing a messiah. Latching onto a newer idea and it's incredible how nobody can see it. This holy war over this dopy rig, we're all prof rig serfs of Christos over here. Lardasses created in the mind of forgers. Ripoffs, all of them. The lies they feed all of US are tubular and I could be stuck here until at least June. Are vests still in style at home? You know, those awesome sweater vests? When I get home I'm scooping up a bunch of them and some user vet jeans and taking Jess out to the planetarium to propose. Actually it just occurred to me, we'll see about the pimp vests though since June is lasagna month according to mom's tradition. I'll probably gain 20lbs when I first get home and look like a planet floating around the sun. Just elated and elevated. Elastic around the mid rift too. With onion rings orbiting around me. Basically all June is anal gas. So roar anus! I swear I'm not drunk as I write this now. They try to teach us in church that the answer is in what sustains us, but they don't teach us that in this new age, the answer is in what sustains us. I'm so proud of you, baby bro. You found a girl who can make you laugh; she's a funny little wench, isn't she? I can't put into words how much I love her and how happy I am for both of you. You are so gifted and incredibly smart. Laughter is the most important thing in the world. Listening to you and your friends talk sometimes I almost have peed myself. Okay, when I was drunk I definitely have urinated on

myself. But if you tell anyone I'll deny it completely and say that you sent this letter to yourself. God I wish I was as smart as you sometimes. One day when you are a doctor, get yourself a house by the water and ride it out. I know you were worried when I joined the Marines at first but I kept telling you that it's just sea nerve. When I get out, I'll start an organic food restaurant for you. "Meal by Bro, no gmo, FUCK lab embryo." You like my slogan? I'm a rapper now. Flo Rida, no Flow ride. Where my pills at? Just kidding. I'd go into therapy before I'd take antidepressants. Ain't got no PTSD and won't let 'em hurt my heart. Haha, look at me now. Ramble Boy!

How's Montana doing? Crap. Before I mentioned it earlier but I forget I need to tell you something very important. This is about my lovely Jess. I've finally found the one Teddy. I've been holding back from you and I'm sorry. She's a bit older than me, actually a lot and apparently she's been watchin' me for a while, while I was at home. Love is a funny thing. First you don't really know these new feelings, then you seem to lose track of time and all you do is focus on this new person. It becomes an obsession. I've been through others in my past and you know this, but I've never been so sure of this one in my life, Teddy. At first I wasn't sure if it was the alcohol talking, I kept blamin' these feelings on the brews. No different than anyone, I think. I'm sure I'm not the first who blamed it all on them. But when I sobered up, something kept telling me she was different, special, and not to fuck it up and lose her. So I followed my instinct. You've got to meet her, Graham. I mean, baby bro, you know me. For me to tell you what this girl has done to me, you know it's the real deal. When I met her, she made me want to run down from your frat house across from the Capitol all the way to St. Peters Church across from our house where we grew up screaming, "Jess, you it baby! I'll never let you go. Where have you been all my life?" I quit late LA life because of her. Well, not quite at all. I didn't at first, but eventually I realized she was the answer and once you find it, Teddy, don't ever lose sight of it. Keep this to yourself though, Teddy. Also say hi to Nerds for me. You might be a bit young to remember this but he reminds me of that kid from *Family Ties*. Still though, you don't have to have family ties to be one of the family. The military drops me a bonus payment November 5th. Just remember, remember if I don't get him a birthday gift by then to remind me, would ya? Friends like him come once in a lifetime, don't ever forget that. I worry at times. I feel like the day he finally gets laid he's going to literally explode. Or will get the girl pregnant and she will end up giving birth to a ten-year-old from all his backup and neuroses.

It is sleight shamanic Teddy to go outside

sometimes and stare at the sky. It doesn't compare to that mushroom Dutch Chi I drank when I was in Amsterdam on my short leave, that was truly eye-opening. The stars were like crystals in the sky and I felt like I could swim around in them. They say that during the Big Bang we were all part of that tiny singularity. Do you think that means long after I'm gone that you can look up to the sky, in those crystals, and see a part of me? I hope if that's the case that part of me will be kept in time.

You can't angrily bend men if peace is your mission. The only law to it all is karma for sure, like the precession of the equinox. I know a lot of what I'm saying doesn't make a lot of sense to you now Teddy, but just think of it like this. Last year you couldn't pay me in whores and cookie dough to try and understand what I've just told you. It's all happening now, can you feel it? God I wish I was as smart as you sometimes. All right, enough of these mail talk wits. Can't wait to see you, broski. I did a search and I noticed that your favorite band The Rising is playing at The Hill. Kicking off their How We Fell Off Atlantis tour December 21–24 at 7 p.m. and December 25th they're doing a show at 9 p.m. I should be home by then and I guess it's a special party for late-risers on Christmas. Let me know if you're interested. Guess they have one final plan for me before I get my release. Just so you know, I always keep my writing on

me. Until I mail. Always. I'll leave you with this, Teddy. Peter: 1: 19-21: "Continue until the day star rises in your hearts."

Semper Fi,

James

"Who's Teddy?" Jean asked as he returned with the refreshment time.

"Me. Teddy...Graham.." I was for some reason unreasonably annoyed that Jean didn't know my brother's nickname for me.

"When did you brother get engaged?" he asked.

"I need air," I said.

We walked around Washington DC with vodka OJs in Coke cans because, well, the police are stupid. Wait, what in the hell did I just read? My frat house wasn't across from the Capitol; it was near Dupont. Also, the church I rarely went to at home was St. Thomas and not St. Peters. When did James become religious? My favorite band was not The Rising. That boy band came out after he'd left for Syria. Yes, the public shot down the idea of going to war with Syria a few years ago, but the government was still deploying people to that area. I know this because my brother got his orders to go there. If he wasn't in Syria, where did they send him? Drugs in Holland now? *Engaged?* Since when did he even have a girlfriend? This guy wrote the book on how to have other women bring women over for him. Wasn't he just telling me about how he'd wanted to be a bartender at a strip club? Also he *chose* to go into the Marine Corps; he got into med school and business school. Big bro could run circles around me. Could have run circles around me. I'm feeling sick again. What was that letter about?

You want a physicist to speak at your funeral. You want the physicist to talk to your grieving family about the conservation of energy, so they will understand that your energy has not died. You want the physicist to remind your sobbing mother about the first law of thermodynamics; that no energy gets created in the universe, and none is destroyed. You want your mother to know that all your energy, every vibration, every Btu of heat, every wave of every particle that was her beloved child remains with her in this world. You want the physicist to tell your weeping father that amid energies of the cosmos, you gave as good as you got.

And at one point you'd hope that the physicist would step down from the pulpit and walk to your brokenhearted spouse there in the pew and tell him that all the photons that ever bounced off your face, all the particles whose paths were interrupted by your smile, by the touch of your hair, hundreds of trillions of particles, have raced off like children, their ways forever changed by you. And as your widow rocks in the arms of a loving family, may the physicist let her know that all the photons that bounced from you were gathered in the particle detectors that are her eyes that those photons created within her constellations of electromagnetically charged neurons whose energy will go on forever.

And the physicist will remind the congregation of how much of all our energy is given off as heat. There may be a few fanning themselves with their programs as he says it. And he will tell them that the warmth that flowed through you in life is still here, still part of all that we are, even as we who mourn continue the heat of our own lives.

And you'll want the physicist to explain to those who loved you that they need not have faith; indeed, they should not have faith. Let them know that they can measure, that scientists have measured precisely the conservation of energy and found it accurate, verifiable and consistent across space and time. You can hope your family will examine the evidence and satisfy themselves that the science is sound and that they'll be comforted to know your energy's still around. According to the law of the conservation of energy, not a bit of you is gone; you're just less orderly. Amen.

– Aaron Freeman.

CHAPTER 4

So, tell me. Is there some tacky rule of law that funerals have to be on rainy days? I appreciate the allusion to my all-too-familiar hangover and how I feel inside, but couldn't it have just been a slightly nicer…you know what, on second thought, a sunny day probably would have been unbearable for my head right now. Maybe this is how they forge through the whiskey whines in Ireland and funneling fosters in Great Britain. No, wait, that's Australia. I can't seem to think very clearly right now. At least the brothers gave us some Adams Ales to sneak into the service in ginger ale bottles. I could tell Jean is worried about my boozing but he isn't going to say anything, least not for a little while. Good. I have bought myself a part-time enabler. I intend to be numb when President Lilac Northinly comes up to me and asks me to say a few words. I still don't understand why they would honor someone who killed himself? I plan on rehashing this speech that my history teacher in twelfth grade, Mr. Rosibuild, gave; I don't know why it stuck in my mind.

The funeral service was tedious and drawn-out. Time flies when you're having drunk. I felt like a photocopy of a human being sitting in my own skin watching them lower my best friend into the ground. I couldn't help but feel that I wanted to protect him just this one time. It must be so dark and cold in the ground all by himself. But there was nothing I could do. I felt myself start to well up but I couldn't allow myself to cry. Crap, I was almost out of the ginger ale and I couldn't get up. We were in the front row.

"Thank you all so much for coming out today. Please take your seats and welcome. Of all the benefits that come with being the President, the one that swells me with the most pride is being able to command the strongest military the world has ever known," she began.

Wait, what about Rome, Greece, Egypt; weren't they a much larger force? What about the army that took out King Leonidas in the movie 300? Hiccup with a little vomit tinge. No big deal. Head in my hands, damn it. Do better, Graham.

"Did someone pass out? Oh, I'm sorry. Are you okay, Graham? Are you feeling a bit faint?" She paused and looked toward the camera as if delivering an Oscar-winning line. "Here, have some water. This is Graham Newsdon, everybody. It's okay; he's had a rough few days and just needed some water. No, it's okay. Send the nurses and paramedics away. He's here to receive a medal for his brother, who we just lost trying to save his team in a terrorist act," she went on.

Wait, what now?

"Now, due to national security," she continued, "I'm sure you understand that we can't go into more detail than that. You know, I had this speech prepared but under these circumstances I'm going to go a bit off script here. I don't think the usual politics will do. Understand that we are doing everything we can to bring these terrorists to justice. I'd like to call up Graham now, if he's feeling up to it, to accept the Congressional Medal of Honor for his brother, James."

Murdered? I couldn't think straight. I had just gotten used to the idea of suicide. Killed for our country? What was Jean initially talking about? I couldn't deliver my speech if he killed himself; it wouldn't make sense. What was going on?

"Th—thank you, Madam President," I said.

Really? Was that the best I could do?

I spent the next hour in the Oval Office dancing with the finest whiskey from one of those stereotypical crystal decanters they have in the movies for exactly these types of situations. Look at me now, Mom and Dad; I'm drunk at the White House.

"It's a pleasure to meet you, Graham. From what I've heard, your brother spoke an awful lot about you during his time over there," Lilac said.

"Where exactly would 'over there' be? Syria? North Africa?" I returned. I was suppressing my anger a bit, apparently not doing a very good job.

"Slow down, Michael Malloy. At your pace, you might actually pass out this time. How was the spiked ginger ale?" she said.

"How did you know?" I replied.

"Not my first trip to the rodeo. I can spot them a mile away. Regarding your brother, we still bear an active interest in the area in question. What I can tell you is that during the ambush, one of them managed to tag one of the terrorists. We're pursuing that lead. It's a bit like the war on drugs we're fighting here, Graham. We can pinch this guy and he might talk; he might not. But then it goes dead. Or he can lead us to a higher-up. Then we jump in. Shake them up and let them go if they trade up to a higher-up. We don't want the nickel-and-dimes; we follow the rabbit hole all the way down to the puppeteer," she finished. Does she always sound like she's reading from a script?

"So my brother's death meant nothing, then?" Here comes the temper. "Where the *fuck* is his justice? What does that mean? Tag one of them?"

Came off a bit strong there. Secret Service agents started power walking toward me. Oh well. Giant gulp of whiskey down the pipe, in case I needed to make a legendary run for it.

"Hold off, gentlemen. It's okay. He's just had a rough day. He's just displacing. It's not like he thinks I executed his brother. Look, Graham," she said as she took the seat closest to me and tried to put on her best mom face. "I'm not supposed to disclose this, but I can see you're not going to function unless I give you something. Let me try and explain a bit better, but both you and your friend need to keep this to yourselves; this isn't exactly something that we release on the news and talk about on a daily basis," she continued as she took a puff off her electronic cigarette. "Certain people that enter the armed forces test high in certain areas and are consequently brought onto certain, let's call them, teams. Your brother was one of those. Neither of these statements should come as a surprise to you. He had a brilliant mind just like you do; you both come from a gifted family. We're not talking about a game of tag here. Some of the KA-BARs that are issued to these teams are tipped with radioactive isotopes and some keychain knives have tracking devices smaller than the size of a grain of rice coated to the blade. In some missions, the object isn't to take them out; it's to tag. You create a surface-level cut to get this tracking device and isotope in, make it look like you missed a kill stab, then let them get away. Ninety percent of the time, they will either take you to a hospital, to their family, or to their base. It's an acting job, psyops at its finest, for those who can sell it. I can't tell you how we track the isotope, that's top clearance, but that's what I meant by tag. I'm sorry if you thought I was jerking you around." She looked self-satisfied as she took another drag of her fake cigarette.

"Madam President. I just don't understand! Why did they tell Jean it was a suicide and here you're telling me he was killed?" Yeah, I thought it was a good question, too.

"I'm so sorry, Graham, my head's been all over the place today. Your brother's death was a suicide," she said and waited for my reaction before she continued. I held it back so she could go on. "Three of the six lost their lives in the ambush. Your brother took his own life the day after, on base. You met the two surviving Marines today, I believe. They were sitting on either side of you.

"This doesn't make sense. I don't follow, Madam President. Forgive me if this sounds childish, but why did you lie to everybody?" I said.

"This is a bit more difficult to explain, Graham. Please understand that it's better sometimes that people don't hear certain details. Not everybody thinks or processes information the same way and you have to do what's best to guide the mindset of the collective than always be worried about telling the exact truth. Ever hear the phrase, 'A person is smart but a group is stupid'? It's true. The truth is that the public reaction to being one-hundred-percent honest every step of the way is unpredictable and beyond impossibly time-consuming at best. Think about having to explain to different intelligence levels, whereas controlled messages that spread across a broader line are more manageable. Your mother had two children she was responsible for, right? I have 350 million, many of whom have polarizing views. How is it possible to reach out and connect with all of them? Let's use today as an example. Even if I went out there and said your brother took his own life, what difference would that make? What personal business is it but yours and your family's? Also, a portion of the people out there would still think I was full of it and that something sinister happened. Now, look, because of the deaths of this particular team, we had let our allies know that we needed to rebuild the team, as well as build up national pride for our heroes who risk their lives for us. This was done in one fell swoop: what you were just a part of. We didn't lie to you to offend you, Graham. I just didn't have time to reach you before. Plus, seeing your reaction now, how would you have handled this while walking up to the stage?" She paused to take another fake-a-rette drag. "Now, with all that being said, Graham, I have to ask you something incredibly important. In the course of your talking with your brother, did he ever mention a source of writing he was working on?"

"Ma'am?" I quizzed back.

"After his death and the deaths of most of his team members during that unfortunate event, one member found a note in his pillow that said, 'I always keep my writing on me. Until I mail. Always.' We checked his outgoing military e-mail and there was nothing. He didn't mail anything out to you or to anyone in the last year and he was extremely private and always self-involved. At least, that's what the remaining two of the original six seem to suggest."

I shot Jean a quick look but pulled it back when I realized he hadn't read the entire letter from my brother. Although inebriated, I didn't want a room full of Secret Service agents with guns and the President of the United States grilling me about my brother to know that he had not only reached out to me, but that he'd used the same phrase they found in his pillow. She might have noticed that and have drawn attention away from it. Act really drunk.

"Why would you only send a team of six for that long? I just don't understand why this happened to him. Why can't you tell me what happened?" Crap, I think I oversold it.

"Gentlemen, thank you for your time. Graham, if you can think of anything when you're in a better condition and you would like to have a chat, please send me an e-mail. Title it

Code WZ #1526 and it will get delivered directly to me. It's my classified code, so don't share it with anybody. Thank you for your time; I'm sorry for your loss. These men will show you out. We have your brother's belongings to return to you." She turned to leave.

An American flag, a pair of boots, the Congressional Medal, clunky watch, dog tags, and a necklace with some sort of clear rock attached to it is all that James was reduced to. Gone at thirty-three and just another name on the wall in Washington. At least I get to sleep this off on the eight-hour ride back to Mass. Something wasn't sitting quite right with me, but my hangover was starting up and I couldn't focus on re-reading this letter. If I only knew at the time just how intelligent my brother was and how he was able to reach me from the grave, I might have handled this conversation with the President differently.

CHAPTER 5

"I want everything you have on those two kids. I know that drunk one is sitting on something that I just can't put my finger on. Roger, when I said I want it, I mean yesterday," Lilac fumed.

"Right away, Madam President." The Secretary of Defense shuffled out of the room.

It had been a long year for Lilac Northinly, starting with the death of her husband to cancer, then shortly after her twin son and daughter beginning college. Her son went to Syracuse to pursue journalism while her daughter decided to go to Penn State on her first stop toward becoming a vet. Lilac, for the life of her, couldn't understand why her son wanted to enter journalism. She wondered if she could sit back and watch Tommy become one of the vipers that watch her every move, ready to chastise her at a moment's notice. It was obnoxious enough that the correspondents' dinner had just passed a few months ago and that exact subject was brought up by one of them, forcing Lilac to confront it with a big fake smile on her face. This job was starting to get to her. She had noticed her hair had gotten slightly grayer and she was sporting a few more wrinkles than before. It was partially her fault. After Jack died, she dove into work. Yes, the life of the President is already planned out and hectic enough, but she would sit in meetings that she wasn't required to attend, anything to keep her mind going and off her husband.

"Steve, Alex, why don't you give me a minute alone with Jake, okay?" Lilac said to her Secret Service detail.

"No problem, ma'am. We'll be right outside," Alex said.

She waited until they had left and gave the room thirty seconds without sound. She took a deep breath, opened up a new electronic cigarette, and sat down to her old friend.

"Lilac, as your primary advisor, I'm advising you to let this thing with the kid go. It was a tragedy and nobody knows better than I do how important it is to image-manage and possibly spin if need be, but you're chasing a ghost with the Solex boy and his friend. They're just two bright kids who like the sauce a bit. Plus, how exactly would his brother have gotten him secret information, information so secret that you won't even tell me what it's about?" Jake said.

"It's not some magical secret information, Jake. I don't take a message like the one that he left under his pillow lightly. What if he was talking about the top-secret mission; what if he was trying to spill intelligence? You know this country has had a bad case of distrust since the Snowden incident. It takes a lot to build back the public trust and I'm not willing to jeopardize it because I thought this was too minor to look into. The truth is that there is not one day I live when I'm not trying to protect people or do the best possible job I can. Now I'd really love for you to climb on board with this. We'll check the two kids out and if this doesn't pan out, then you can be the first to say I told you so," Lilac finished as she puffed.

"All right, Lilly. That sounds fair enough; just promise me that you're not going to waste your time on some bullshit. God knows we have enough that we have to get through. We also have your re-election to think about; when do you plan on having that conversation?"

"You know that I'm not ready to talk about that yet; not until I know my kids are settled into school, the budget goes through, and this thing with these kids turns up going nowhere."

"What happened to you, Lilly? Remember how this used to be fun for us not so long ago? Every day a new excitement, new challenges; visiting a new place. What changed?" Jake asked.

"Stress. It's like one brick at a time until you have the great pyramids sitting on your back," she replied.

"Madam President." Roger rushed back. "I just got back some information out of the DoD from our contacts handling the Newsdon kid. It seems that he took a few days he had for himself between missions and flew out to Europe. We're still trying to pin down where he went, but it looks like somewhere in Germany."

"How is it even possible that he made it there?" Lilac puffed.

"He had a few different passports, undercover aliases, and he's been trained to disappear and re-appear on cue. What's the big deal with this kid, anyway?" Roger said.

"I don't take kindly to Marines leaving their base to go on benders halfway around the world. Are you sure that you combed through his things before you gave them to his brother? There was no writing?" she asked, a tinge of pleading in her voice.

"None. Even if there was, why wouldn't the kid be able to talk to his brother?" Roger questioned.

"It's not that he can't; it's that he went out of his way to make sure his writing would not be found. When we found that letter under his pillow, it was part of a book; it was numbered. He kept a journal. When we turned his section over, we couldn't find the journal. There's something about this that I'm not very happy about. Roger, where is the information on the two boys?" Lilac said.

"There's nothing here, really. Graham has a urinating in public ticket and there's nothing on

Jean; his family has kept him clean. What exactly are we looking for?"

"Secondary location where mail goes? A PO box, maybe? Anything that looks unusual."

"The kid is broke, Lilac. He doesn't have a PO box. Why don't we leave Jean out of this, or have you forgotten the family's considerable donations to your election campaign?"

"He's got a point, Lilly," said Jake. "This is going nowhere. Now please go change into the blue dress so we can meet the Ambassador for dinner. We're going to be late."

"I don't like this one bit," Lilac said as she headed off to change her clothes. "I'm not through with this. I want to know where he went in Germany." What she really needed was Jack. Jack used to keep her focused and calm in a way that she seldom found able to do anymore. He would know what to do about this situation with Germany. He would always challenge Lilac's decisions and make her see a new light; they were the perfect couple. If Lilac was going to have to do this on her own, she was going to first have to make it through dinner with the Spanish Ambassador.

"Let's say you're sleeping and someone lights up a 600 watt light bulb next to you. The first thing you're going to do is shield your eyes. Why? Because someone who's more intellectually brilliant that tries to wake up someone who has been sleeping their whole life will be offended. Secondly they will be angry because they don't want to have to think."

—Jordan Maxwell

CHAPTER 6

Nothing cures a hangover like a coffee and Baileys. Seriously. We got back to Mass at the Devil's Hour. I was drained, but eight hours of sleep when you're used to five can seriously fix that. I forgot to take a glass of milk with Ibuprofen the night before. When you drink, alcohol irritates your stomach lining, so having a cup of milk coats it. I was paying the price now. I had to fight through it. NP just got in and I needed a fresh view.

"You really need to learn to lock your door. What if I was a cannibal? Mother of God, look at you. It's a good thing you can lose up to eighty percent of your liver and survive because you're probably pushing it at this point," NP said.

Crap. I must have fallen asleep again. Fortunately for me, he's right. He's referring to the fact that we each have a bile duct and because of that we can donate half of our liver and it will straight up regrow itself. It's the only organ that will do that and I bet we evolved this starfish-like feature on our alcohol filter just for people like me.

"All I've got left in my wallet is a few first presidents. I guess you can have them as dowry for not taking advantage of me," I said jokingly.

"Dowry? You mean like I give you an ox and a sheep and you give me Rosette? Also, I believe you mean tenth presidents," he said.

"What?" I replied.

"George Washington was this country's tenth president. We became an independent country in 1776, correct? George Washington became the president in 1789, right? What happened for those thirteen years? Pants off dance off?" he asked. "By the way, I saw you on TV. You looked like your idea was to cure a hangover with a new hangover. I mean, really. National TV and you get up on the podium and make these faces. Just priceless. Also, wait, sorry, more important. Your brother's death wasn't a suicide?" he asked.

"Actually, according to the President it was, but they didn't need to air that out so they played politics and said he died with the rest who died in the ambush," I said. It sounded even more confusing coming out of my mouth.

"Politics as usual," he replied.

"Except something didn't sit well with me. They asked me about some writing from my brother. He wrote me an e-mail from an unknown computer and not from his military e-mail. There's so much crazy in it that I don't know what to make of it and I'm beginning to wonder if I even knew this guy to begin with. Anyway, in the e-mail, he wrote that he keeps his writing 'on me at all times,' 'until I mail,' and 'always,' which makes sense, until the President told me that they found a note in his pillow saying the same thing. I didn't tell them he contacted me or used that phrase. She told me they checked his outgoing mail and found nothing and I'm assuming they found no stacks of paper being sent out, and traced his steps best as they could. Anyway, she gave me this code to e-mail the White House if I have any further information; it'll go directly to her."

"Interesting," he replied.

"Why is that interesting?"

"You found it interesting. I can't find it interesting? Let me share with you a few rules I live by, Graham. It takes the confusion out of things. I promise you, I've never been led wrong. L. Fletcher Prouty said that things don't happen by accident in the government. Two, always follow the money trail. Remember that movie, *Vanilla Sky*, we saw the other day? 'My father wrote about this in his book. Chapter 1, Page 1, Paragraph 1: What is the answer to 99 out of 100 questions? Money.' There once was this inventor who went up to Caesar with a form of bendable glass. Honestly, it was completely malleable. He threw the cup on the ground and it bent inward instead of shattering. Caesar promptly had him put to death because he was afraid he was going to usurp the value of gold. To this day, the consistency of how it was done has never been duplicated. Three, words are never chosen, used, or created by accident. If you don't fully understand what it means, you have to look into it because you're not looking at it the right way. Fourthly, don't ever believe the stories that are sold to you by the papers and the news that are collectively colluded on. The news has advertisers that pay their salaries. Everything on TV is fake or false. Cartoons are fake, sitcoms, and soap operas. They all have commercials that pay to keep them on TV. It's the same with the news. Remember when I said that my father and grandfather were both thirty-year-plus copy editors and producers for a very big mainstream news source. After the obligatory 'Boogeyman Claims Three More in the Park Tonight' story used to scare the shit out of your ass and get you to stay in your house, they go to break and it's a Coca Cola commercial. Now coca is derived from the coca plant, and cola comes from kola, which is the kola nut from the same plant, which flavored the original drink. They also used to literally put bits of cocaine in the drink in the early 1900s. Where did they get the idea to do that? In 1863, a Frenchman named Angelo

Mariani created a wine called Vin Mariani, vin being the French word for wine. He thought it a good idea to add some cocaine to it. It was so catchy in the Absinthe community that it spread like wildfire and eventually found its way to Pope Leo XIII and Pope Saint Pius X, who carried it on them in hip flasks like magic spells of RPG characters. Leo XIII even went so far as to award a Vatican gold medal to Mariani. To this day, Coca Cola still imports coca leaves into this country through a processing lab called the Stepan Company. Now let me ask you a question. You're H20 News and Coca Cola pays you millions of dollars a year in advertising. Are you going to report this story to everyone?" he finished excitingly.

"How do you know all of this?" I asked

"I tickled the CEO with a feather while he was tied up in my torture chamber. He told me everything."

"I don't have time for all that crap. I need your help, NP. I need you to read this letter and tell me what you think. I'm running out of ideas here. I printed a few copies when I was in DC the day before the funeral; you can have one."

"That's probably the smartest thing you've ever done. I'll work on this tonight." His eyes grew wide.

"Why was that the smartest thing?" I replied.

"From what you just told me, they don't believe he hasn't contacted you. You're lucky you opened it before you went there, because the NSA is probably now tapping your computer and monitoring your e-mails. I would not use your computer. Talk to you kids later; the super team needs me," he finished as he disappeared out the door and down the hallway.

"What is he talking about?" Hannah asked.

"Well, when Captain America retires, he wants to be the first one that they look for when trouble comes. So, as long as his costume is not an argyle sweater tucked into his underwear—" I trailed.

"I meant the NSA thing. Seriously, Graham?" She rolled her eyes.

"Read this," I said. As I lay there looking at my girl reading the letter my brother wrote me, I couldn't help but realize how lucky I was to have someone who loved me unconditionally. Her gorgeous green eyes and long brown hair. The way she freckles up a bit when she hits the sun. Her sense of humor was so potent that I felt myself choking from laughing at times. My attention drifted toward the television and wouldn't you know, Blur Slanders was on. The remote was across the room. I was too lazy to get up. NP left him on and he's talking about the latest country we are deploying to and why we need to rise up against the machine. Throw in some obligatory Anonymous movement references and you've got your standard show. It's incredible the didactic difference between what is said on regular TV and what is shown on TRAM TV. I've heard one of NP's Adderall talks about the elite and their desire for population control but how is that going to happen exactly if we need to occupy the world? After about ten minutes of just lying together, she spoke up.

"When did your brother get a girlfriend?"

"I was trying to figure," I said, as she cut me off and started speaking rapid-fire.

"Also, why does he talk about The Rising? You hate The Rising. Me and Rose are the ones who love them. Least I hope you're not into a boy band that rides out in fire trucks spraying water on everyone and themselves. God, it's so hot. Also, they are not playing at the Hill; they're going to be at the Square that week. What was he talking about?" she finished in a single breath.

As I went for round two, a hot chocolate and Goldschlager (don't judge until you've tried it), I let this roll around in my head. I finished it up and cuddled with my girl. Luckily, cocoa and cinnamon is an acceptable breath to have. I was drifting off to sleep and was at that stage where things start to not make sense, but you roll with it anyway. I was balancing chemical equations and when I got them right, they would jump off the paper and start dancing. Don't judge me. Suddenly, I was sucked back into this reality when we were startled by NP kicking the door down. He wasn't kidding: if he was a cannibal,

I'd have no legs by now.

"Get up!" he said, his face flushed.

"Damn it, NP! You know, man, what if I had a bad heart?" I said more than a little annoyed at being ripped out of my semi-alpha-wave dream set.

"But, we have to talk," he pleaded.

"I bet you have tortellini-sized hernias all over your—" I started before I was cut off.

"I don't think this is a normal letter," he triumphed. Big deal. I'd already come to that conclusion on my own.

"Congratulations. You didn't need to shave months off my life for that. I already know it's not. It makes no sense. Also, he went off the deep end and killed himself," I finished as I tried to get myself back into an acceptable pass-out position.

"No, you insufferable bunghole. Listen. This is not a normal letter. It makes no sense. So I did some digging and I found some consistency within the inconsistency," he said.

"Am I still asleep? What are you saying to me?" I replied, now more than a little annoyed. You know how in the cartoons when they open the closet and it's packed so tight everything pours out and covers them from head to toe? That would be me with anti-anxiety medicine when I'm around this kid.

"What did I literally just get finished saying not even an hour ago? 'Nothing is an accident.'

Words are never used by accident; everything is worded and placed exactly where it belongs. Look at his first main paragraph. PITCHERS of Adam's Ale, that sweet AMBROSIA. Hard to be a CRAB, RETRO BEETLES, the ORIGINAL BEETLE. TWIN, VIRGIN night? Greatest Of All Time? CUPID, SHOT, ARROW." He smiled and then quickly frowned when he realized that nobody thinks like him and he would have to bring it down a level to reach others.

"Fascinating. It sounded to me like, 'It's hard to be angry when you have pitchers of everybody's favorite beer while listening to the Beatles, before Yoko's vagina ruined them on twin virgin night. Come on down for the greatest night ever. Get shot through the heart.' Actually, it sounds like it could be the new Adams Ale commercial. Actually, it sounds like a pretty awesome night," I nervously half laughed because I thought it was funny, while the other half remembered my brother was no longer on this side of the white wall.

"Look closer, Simba. He deliberately misspelled the Beatles twice. There was a fifth member of the Beatles named Stuart Sutcliffe. He played with the band in Germany while they were getting their Malcolm Gladwell ten-thousand hours on. He stayed back in Germany when they started up and then mysteriously died of a brain hemorrhage. They never replaced him. Apparently, there was another member,

Pete Best, who was replaced by Ringo, but there's nothing crazy about that. Except for the part that Ringo was put in the band. Ringo sucked. Point is, this has nothing to do with the Beatles." He stopped short of popping a blood vessel in his neck.

"You make me drink—you know that?" I said. He barely let me get that sentence out before he hot-air ballooned another whopper.

"He capitalizes the g, the o, the a, and the t. Cupid-shot arrow? You know how I always bust on Rosette because of her fascination with horoscopes. No comments, Hannah. What if this is encoded? Look. Ambrosia pitcher is the story of Aquarius. Legend had it that Zeus saw a young boy on Earth and wanted him for himself because back in this time it was acceptable to have an underage boy as a sex slave, even if you were a worshipped god. He gave this boy's father a herd of animals, which pleased the father because, well, I guess the father liked animals more than his own child. The boy was Zeus's servant and would serve him ambrosia out of this pitcher. One day he got fed up with being the gods' plaything so he poured the pitcher out, which flooded the Earth for days. Zeus was pissed and was about to take vengeance, but in a random moment of reflection, I guess of self-realization, that what he was doing was naughty, he immortalized this child as the constellation Aquarius in the act of him pouring the water out," he finished. Almost made me feel bad I didn't steal and bring home an oxygen canister from the teaching hospital.

"Right. So Hannah, remember about a month ago when you were telling me that you were worried that our kids might smoke pot one day?" I said with a straight face that almost cracked with each word.

"Shut up." She laughed.

"NP, next time they have a Congressional meeting about the dangers of rap music, take out an index card with this story and read it in your best bedtime-story voice. Give me a break," I said.

"The next one was hard for me because of the Beatles thing but then I thought, what if he meant the spelling intentionally? Crab, retro beetles, the original beetle. Well the crab is the sign of Cancer, but in Egyptian culture it was the scarab. You even get the word crab out of scarab. You see it everywhere in the hieroglyphics. The scarab is the 'original' beetle. The twin virgin? That's just Gemini, the twins Castor and Pollux. Pollux's father was Zeus, the unregistered sex offender, remember? You may have heard of their famous twin sister, Helen of Troy. Virgin is Virgo. G, o, a, t the GOAT is Capricorn. Cupid-shot arrow, the archer, Sagittarius."

He then paused and surveyed the room and smiled as he saw the face I was wearing. I was starting to feel that fight-or-flight feeling in my stomach. Just the thought of my brother trying to reach out to me with a letter from the dead was enough to make me want to drink myself back to sleep. I think I had a flask of blackberry brandy from last week's party still in the freezer.

"So you're saying that he put symbolism into the note. Do you know what you're asking me, NP? On one hand, either James went crazy before he took his own life and wrote a slightly wacky note, or this is a bizarre codex. If you were in my slippers, what would you think?" I pleaded, almost hoping he would take it all back and come up with a brand new and reasonable way to explain what he'd just said.

"We've been friends since we were in middle school, G. What have I always said to you? Keep an open mind. Fight your inner desire to block out what you don't agree with. It's called cognitive dissonance. It's why people dismiss one person after a slight disagreement but in the same turn give another person a ton of free passes. It's their biases. The best thing you can do is be self-aware of your own. While you think about that, one last thing: that Halloween when you dressed up as a lion; do you still have pictures?" he asked. I could feel a finale coming. I knew I shouldn't play into this. I shouldn't get that picture so that he could layer another scoop onto this rising shit sundae. Unfortunately, his mental process was and always will be intoxicatingly more interesting than my alcoholic think processing.

"I should. That was the last year my parents were together. Hold up a sec," I said.

Brandy is a funny thing. I now know why Oscar Wilde painted characters of egregious, fat, northern English aristocrats with cheesy monocles and Teddy Roosevelt mustaches sipping in the winter while they talked about the best way to count their money and the last time they were able to see their penises over their stomachs. It warms you up immediately. Seriously, I felt like I was having a sulfite reaction to wine. As I opened the box, the pictures were surprisingly sitting right at the top. I'm not going to go into the psychological implication that I must have re-visited them but couldn't remember when. I flipped through them looking for the ice storm my brother was talking about and the torn-up costume. Being buried in our backyard sandbox. These were just generic pictures. I was starting to get all hot and bothered as they say, and not in a good way. Seriously, the brandy was lighting me on fire and this letter was starting to piss me off.

"So we are in agreement, then," he yelled after a few minutes and hearing me escape an annoyed sound from the other room. "Look here; he even says he would take you to see The Rising. You don't even like The Rising. I mean, who the hell does?"

"Excuse me, but shut up, Nerds," Hannah

politely interjected.

"Look, the point is that the name of their tour isn't even the How We Fell Off Atlantis tour. It's called the Raining in the Light tour. I mean the oral pun. Listen up to the sky. He's telling you something here," NP said to us.

"You're officially saying this letter is some code we have to crack?" I posed, half hoping as a last ditch effort he would retract everything he'd just said.

"I'm saying this letter is illusory. I'm saying he knew he was in trouble one way or another, so he stashed his secrets in a letter. I know. How tacky, right? I'm thinking that this is deeper than I've figured out so far. I didn't recognize it at first, but when he mentioned my name I started looking at it a little more closely. C'mon, we've got to get to the library," NP said.

"Why not stay here? I've got a computer," I said, half hoping to parlay my laziness and drinks into a night in.

"There's no bar at the library. Plus that four-year-old thing you call a laptop is probably being monitored at this point. Also going to need access to books and lots of them at the drop of a hat," he concluded as he pulled me to my feet.

I had to admit, it sounded absolutely insane, but come on. Even when you know something sounds crazy, there is a tiny part of you that has an intuition that you go with. I had been fighting that feeling since he'd started talking ten minutes before. A lot of the letter didn't sound much like him, like the brother I knew. Although this sounded more up NP's alley, I had to do something. I had absolutely no idea how right he was and how deep this rabbit hole was about to take us.

CHAPTER 7

We got to the library and set up shop in one of the back corner quiet rooms. We brought these dry-erase boards that I was using as a musculoskeletal and circulatory map. I hadn't erased them since undergrad. Jean called and said he would meet us there with Rosette. He had some business-class BS to finish up and Rosette just got finished at her swim meet. Speaking of which, my head was still swimming. What the hell does astrology have to do with anything and why did he bring up that Halloween?

"I'll let you set up with Hannah. On the walk over, something came up in my mind. There's a book I need to grab. I'll be right back. No, wait, I'll set up the board. No wait, I'll be right back." Typical self-conversation as NP bolted off.

I swear, he needed to be medicated. I sat down and started re-reading my brother's e-mail. This was the first time I'd actually taken a look at it since the frat house. Open mind, NP said. How exactly does one do that?

"You okay, sweetie? You know I love you and I'm here for you always, right?" Hannah said lovingly.

The love I have for this woman. When she's not driving me bananas. One of these days, she will be Mrs. Mine forever. If she doesn't first chop me into pieces when I'm sleeping.

"Found it. First, let's set up a part of the board by zodiac sign. I don't think your brother placed anything out of order or meant anything by accident. He started with Aquarius and ended with Leo," NP said.

"What about the other signs that aren't in here?" Hannah inquired.

"For now let's just start with the outliers he set up for us because they are in order time-wise. If you read into it your way, they jump all over the place. Plus, he left some signs out," he retorted as he went to work.

"As if this isn't an acid trip to begin with," she replied.

"Wait, lets at least see this out. I mean, it does sound nuts but so far it isn't beyond comprehension." I would quickly regret those words.

"I've been waiting twenty-two years to hear you start talking like that. Come to Butthead," he said in his best impression of the Mike Judge character.

"You know, the line I'm giving you is thinner than your chances with Rosette," I said, laughing.

"Me what?" Rosette chirped as she walked in.

"You cut me deep, Shrek. Uncalled for. Rose, my love. You up to speed?" he asked.

"Yep. I got the e-mail Pierce sent me. Let me look at the letter. We got copies?" she asked. I did mention that being the jock of the group, everything was last names for Rosette, didn't I?

"I'll go make more. NP, you sent this to Rosette before you came to us?" Hannah attacked.

"Well, I knew you were going to come with me to the library once you saw the light in this," NP replied.

"I hope this place has a snack machine. I feel like I need to regulate my sugar after all of this; I can't think straight," Hannah replied.

"I got it, Husker. I'll get you a candy bar, too. I still need to walk off this lactic acid. I'm starting to cramp up a bit. Shows me for skipping swim for a few days," Rosette said.

"You know, it's ironic that you mention that," NP baited.

"What are you talking about? Diabetes?" I said.

"Well, since you asked, type 1 and 2 diabetes is the body's sugar mismanagement. See, the islets of Langerhans in your pancreas release insulin to regulate and handle the breakdown of sugar. I don't just mean direct sugar, but things like white breads and complex carbs, which get broken down into sugar, and if they're not used up—for example, pasta—they get converted into energy by Rosette before a swim meet and, instead, by Graham ordering pizza drunk at 2 a.m. while playing golf on the PlayStation. Your body won't burn them up; instead, they get broken down into glucose, sugars, and stored as fats. Bad habits like this down the road lead to type 3 diabetes," he said.

"What would that be exactly?" Hannah said.

"Type 3 diabetes. Also known as Alzheimer's," he said quietly.

"Wait. Shut up. That's not true, is it?" I asked. I could sense my regret for saying that as I was saying it.

"This is exactly the problem with how they are training doctors in this country. They train you how to medicate, not how to think, and it's because pharmaceutical companies are the number-one lobbyists in the US, at least by more than a billion dollars. Over oil, special interests, etc. You're only listening to me now because we're best friends and you still think I'm full of shit. Cancer, for example. They treat it with poison radiation. Treating cancer with radiation is like a hostage negotiator treating a hostage situation with a bomb. The terrorists will die, but so do the innocents around them. Also, it doesn't guarantee that more terrorists won't come back again to try and hijack the same place. However, there are at least twenty clinical studies that show that THC cures all different types of cancer. That it just kick-starts the healthy mitochondria back up and causes cancer cells to commit suicide. Tangentially, it has been shown to stop all symptoms of Crohn's disease, which after a night of drinking and your morning bathroom dumps, Graham, I wonder if you don't have an early onset case of. It's also been shown to kill MRSA, relieve intra-ocular nerve pressure from glaucoma, bring appetites back in AIDS patients and people that unfortunately choose to go through radiation, and it also helps with pain. It's still illegal due to economics; it would turn the current cancer treatment system over and cost the pharma companies a ton of money, yet all this is undeniable. Regarding the Alzheimer's bit, where would you like this to come out exactly: in the mainstream news? Give me a break. The news that cuts to commercial and every single one is advertising a drug product? Follow the leader. Sugar resistance in the brain, which eventually damages the hippocampus, is also aided by inflammation of arteries. Where are the memories stored? We're talking about brain damage here. They say things like to do crossword puzzles and write with your non-dominant hand because it'll open up new neural pathways. Bullshit. This doesn't repair a damaged brain. If your computer has some internal damage, the techie doesn't tell you, 'Oh, just keep using it; maybe try this program over and over again. It'll work itself out.' The problem with Alzheimer's is that the only way you can confirm it is postmortem, when you can cut into the person's head because, well, it's not polite to chop into a person's head while they're alive. Even if they think they are a squid," NP finished.

"Well, is there any proof of this?" Another regretful question, courtesy of yours truly. I was rethinking my oxygen-can heist.

"Why has no US president died of cancer since Ulysses S. Grant? Do you think that's a little weird that the number-two killer in America that's supposedly impossible to get rid of has claimed none of the presidents in the last 130 years which, incidentally, was when the study of parasites took off? Why do they still have the Jerry Lewis telethon for the cure for muscular dystrophy when it has been proven to be a selenium deficiency in the body? One day you won't have me here to guide you, sweet G. Wake up, my friend." He laughed as he jumped from topic to topic. I was actually rather used to it by now.

"You will be around forever; do not upset me like that. Wait, now that you mention it, I vaguely remember reading something once in undergrad," I said.

"Sounds like all of frat America. That's some good work," NP laughed.

"You are on fire today, aren't you? Listen, I mean, I remember studying about diabetes in pre-med and seeing an article by some doctor who was trying to make the case that overweight diabetic women had a greater chance of having autistic babies because of complications with sugar during fetal brain development," I said.

"Also, look at the charts of these diabetic women. They carry double the chance of Alzheimer's as a regular person," he said as he folded his arms.

"Do I get a say in that? I nearly peed my pants when I read what he said about you, Pierce. Oh man. Newsdon, your brother was really good at painting a mental picture, wasn't he?" Rosette said.

"Painting a mental picture. Painting a mental picture," NP repeated as his eyes grew wide.

"That's what I said, Rain Man. Do you have something to add?" Rosette quipped.

NP fumbled around a copy of the letter, making small markings and generally looking like he was performing open-heart surgery on a cat. I could see Hannah in the corner debating whether or not to open her candy bar after everything that was just said. After a few moments, NP shot up and scared us half to death.

"Rose enters with the divine inspiration," he said.

"What are you talking about?" she asked sheepishly.

"A picture, of his mind," he said.

With that, NP created a separate section on the board, away from the zodiac. Going back and forth from the e-mail to the board, he put up the following:

Don't really know these new feelings Then you seem to lose track of time All you do is focus on this new person It becomes an obsession Brainy pesters Rise spy banter Inside the binary gland Mmmmkay Warzone conditions Sleep deprivation Lack of food Feeling like you're up to your neck in water. He then sat down for a few minutes, looked at the paper again, then did some more brow-furrowing. Then he pulled out his phone, looked for something, and then ran to a section in the library and started riffling through books.

"Newsdon, active reminder why *not* having children is a better life decision," Rosette replied.

"Rose, as soon as you drop the act and admit that you're going to end up with so many kids you're going to have a zipper instead of a C-scar, the better off we all will be," I shot at her.

"You know, having your head up your ass is a pre-existing condition? Luckily, with our wonderful new healthcare, you can't be denied if you ever want to get that surgery option looked at," she replied. Well done, Rose.

NP must have found what he was looking for. Without saying a word, he came back to the board and in different colors added *Ladies Entertainers & Politicians, Army of pets, Easter and Halloween*, just as Jean was walking in.

"Que c'est il passé?" Jean asked.

"I think we're watching the birth pains of artificial intelligence," I replied.

A minute or two went by. NP looked at the board, then one final time at the letter. He calmly put the marker down, looked over to all of us, and made a few bullet points on the back of the piece of paper. Then he took a huge deep breath, which I've never seen him do before; it kind of startled me actually.

"We have to talk about what your brother knew," he deadpanned.

"You're making me nervous here," I replied.

"This is going to take a little while to explain to you, to all of you. God, I'm so stupid I can't believe I initially missed it. I mean, I've only known about this sort of thing for—" I cut him off. I hate when he dances around information.

"NP!" I yelled

"I'm certain your brother was a trained assassin," NP replied.

"Quoi?" said Jean.

"You've heard of the Manchurian Candidate, right?" said NP.

"You mean like mind-programming people and them doing things then not knowing what they did or to who or being able to control it or remember it?" I asked.

"More or less," NP replied.

"Okay, fine. THIS IS WHERE I DRAW THE LINE! My brother's death was a suicide and this is bananas. You're making connections where they don't need to be and you're just dragging along this pain. I'm out of here." I was halfway out the library and barely heard NP shout after me. I left them at the library just like that. I was so furious with all of them for playing into this bullshit. Even Hannah. I can't believe she would just sit by and allow for this to go on like that. Then it hit me. I smiled when I realized there was some 7 and 7 waiting for me at home—wouldn't you know, my lucky numbers.

After the twenty-minute walk back, I realized that maybe I'd overreacted slightly. Also, that I should probably apologize to NP. All he did was do what he always does: put together conspiracies. I walked into the apartment and immediately poured myself a concoction and sat down with my brother's stuff. I hadn't looked at it yet, really. I couldn't believe I would never get to see him again. Not sure where he got this watch from; didn't look military-issued. Do the seals even have standard watches? Shit, my drink was empty already. This stuff was like candy. I got up to make another one, forgetting I had this clunky thing in my hand, my thoughts lost in my own mind. As I went to put the watch on the table, I didn't really look where I was putting it and it fell onto the floor upside down. Crap. I poured the rest of my drink and picked the watch up. I hadn't noticed it before but there was a carving on the plate. Looked like a steering wheel with the word *flash* across it where I'm guessing the word Ford should have been, since he owned a Mustang.

I sat down and started watching TV. Crap. I was comfortable again and Blur was back on reruns. Why could I never remember to change the channel? Where the hell was the remote? Had to be among the new mess NP created on my desk when he first came in. I hate not knowing where things are. Does this guy ever shut up? Why is he always on TV? You would think this world was run by homicidal alligators the way he yaps his flap. Where was everybody? I started fumbling with the clunky thing. It was definitely my brother's work. He was quite the non-artist. He tried to draw a picture for my mom one year for Mother's Day and I heard her tell my dad later on that it looked like something he had drawn with his foot. This compelled me to walk away even further from the fact that NP thought that James could put together something so elaborate that I couldn't even wrap my mind around its layers. Yet, from what started off as boredom, I decided to play his game. I did promise NP I would try and be open-minded. Well, minus the earlier borderline explosion. Plus, I was a little fuzzy and lucid. So I wrote down all the things I could think of on a piece of paper:

Flashy Car
Flash Me Out the Driver's-Side Window
Flash and The Furious
Make James's Shitty Ford More Flashy
Flash Fuel
What the fuck is flash fuel?
Drive off in a flash
Flash Drive

I stopped writing. I looked at the paper, looked at the watch, looked at the inscription, looked at the paper again. No freakin' way. I looked closer at the watch. Looked like a regular watch, but there seemed be a slightly loose knob on it. So I screwed it back on. Then, for some reason, I saw NP in my face: "Nothing happens by accident or is a coincidence." So I unscrewed it and the little cover came off and there was a hole into the watch. I stared at it for a minute, trying to collect my thoughts. I grabbed a pair of headphones I found tangled on the floor by the TV and tried to plug them into the watch. They fit perfectly and a light lit up at the top of the watch.

When I say you don't think straight when you're buzzed, you really don't. I must have torn half the house apart when suddenly it occurred to me that I owned external speakers that plug into the computer via flash drive and that I could have used that connector cord the entire time. I was just about to plug it into my computer when I remembered what NP said about my computer being monitored. Instead I took the wire, the watch, poured my 7 and 7 in a 7-Eleven cup with ice because, well again, police are stupid. I was going to break down this letter. It took me to figure it out, not for someone to tell me what to believe, but for me to see it with my own eyes. I guess that's how believing goes for everyone, right? "See it for yourself to believe it." Maybe NP guided me in the right direction, but it's true what they say: you can take a camel to the water, but you can't make him drink. Just then I got a text from Hannah.

Baby, I love you. I'm sorry you got so upset but you really need to come back here. I know it's hard to believe but you have to hear what we've just heard. As it started to rain on me, I kept re-reading a part of the letter in my mind, over and over again. *I hope if that's the case, that part of me will be kept in time. I always keep my writing on me.* He must have meant this watch.

CHAPTER 8

"Well that dinner sucked," Lilac shared with Jake as he shot her a disappointed look.

"What did you expect, Lilly? This dinner wasn't for you and you know that," Jake shot back.

"I suppose not," Lilac said as she fumbled in her purse for the electronic cigarette. Truth was she was getting tired of housing guests she didn't want to, but so is the life of the most powerful woman in the world. It was not that long ago that she'd actually looked forward to having her family with her as she hosted these dinners. But with her husband now gone and her kids shipped off to college, all she really wanted to do was curl up in bed with a glass of Chardonnay and watch her favorite shows. She used to watch *House* regularly and imagine herself as a nurse on the floor, fantasizing about not being in her position of power. All these White House dramas on TV were so boring; the way they trivialized what was happening in the world. Then there was the bipolar way the news went back and forth on how they felt about each decision she made. Half the country loved her, half hated her—what difference did it make what decision she made? Oh, to be twenty-five again and a brand new trial lawyer. The world seemed so much larger then. "What's next on the agenda for tonight?" she asked.

"Well, I think you're off the hook right now. Incidentally, our people were able to trace back James Newsdon's flight. One of his passports was flagged. It appears he flew into Hamburg. The details are still coming in as to where he stayed and where he went, but I'll keep you posted. I don't want you concerning yourself with this right now, Lilly, you've got a very important speech before Congress tomorrow and you need your rest."

"Thank you for that update, Jake. If you don't mind, I think I'm going out for a walk," she replied.

"You got it, Lilly. Incidentally, I left a bottle of Prosecco on your nightstand and made sure *Scrubs* was recorded for you."

"You're too good to me, Jake. Thank you," Lilac said. Truth was she wasn't much of a *Scrubs* fan and Prosecco was one of her least favorite drinks, but Jake sure was trying. It seemed like ever since Jack died Jake had paid extra attention to making sure she was comfortable any way he knew how. Sometimes Lilac wondered if there was something more there, but then that thought disappeared from her consciousness as soon as it entered. It was just something that would never happen.

She ended up deciding to catch some fresh air and going to the Rose Garden. It was one of the only places where she found solace; she was at peace for a brief few moments reflecting on how far she had come in the last ten years. That was until the Secret Service came out and set up in formation around her. Once that happened, she usually called it quits; it somehow became less peaceful with Steve and Alex, the monster linebackers with earpieces, standing eight feet from her.

She decided to take the long way back to her room. She was safe in the White House so the dogs gave her some leeway. She finally was able to let her hair down. Usually when she did that people knew not to bother her with work-related questions; it was her little homage to Bob Dylan as he used to play the same card when he wore his hoodie up.

She sat down on her bed and pulled her computer to her. Checked her WZ1526 account: no e-mails. Damn it! Did she really think he was going to e-mail her back? She lay back on her pillow and wondered how things had come this far. How was she going to micromanage Jake while at the same time getting the answers without revealing too much? Shit. This show isn't as good as my favorite show, she thought to herself as she cracked open the Prosecco and crowned it in one fell swoop. It was a constant battle every day just to find time to pee, let alone if God forbid an actual issue came up. Why couldn't she find peace in her work anymore? Why was it so hard for her to come to work with a smile on her face? She used to be good at faking it and lately she couldn't even seem to do that. More importantly, what had she gotten herself into? When did this get so complicated?

CHAPTER 9

Things were exactly as I'd left them nearly an hour before. Dedicated bunch of lab rats, busy little bees. Before I could even catch my breath and get out what I wanted to tell them, NP hopped in spastically.

"You're a little behind. I have to bring you up to speed," he said.

It's amazing how fluid his brain worked despite his neuroses. While I was gone, it seemed this giant dry-erase board had been turned into a war-strategy room. Also, they somehow located a projector and were able to put the letter up on it. He was crossing off sections of the letter that were decoded.

"We need to first talk about your brother and what they did to him over there," he began.

"Over where?" I said.

"Who knows? Or maybe we'll figure it out. We don't know yet. The key to the beginning of this is right here." He circled the word *Mmmmkay*. Funny. I found that a little out of place, too.

"I don't follow but hit me with it," I replied.

"At first I thought it was regarding the

psychologist from South Park, because I know how you guys used to go around saying that back and forth to each other every time you didn't believe something but wanted to make a point out of it anyway. He's referring to the MK Ultra programming," NP said.

"Non, non. This is just something the wacky people, they like to talk about," Jean jumped in.

"Jean, ne t'offences pas, but I've spent years studying declassified documents, interviews, and listening to experts; things you haven't spent an hour looking into. Please let me go on," NP retorted.

"I didn't know you spoke French," Jean replied.

"I don't. I just memorized 'no offense' so I could say it on you one day. What we're basically talking about here is creating multiple-personality disorders in people. Physically creating dissociative identity disorder. You can train a human being to break down their identity and be open to the suggestive nature of other personalities. Then once they're in, you can mold, manipulate, and train these personalities as you see fit," NP concluded.

"What exactly would the point of that be?" Hannah added.

"Have you ever seen the movie *Zoolander*? It's the same concept, only not as cartoonish." As NP spoke, he would cross off words from the letter as his points became illustrated. Just furthering the horror and the justification that I should have listened to him all along. "You train people in MK by starvation, sleep deprivation, light deprivation, and loud noises. Loud music. During one particular situation, they played Twisted Sister's "We're Not Gonna Take It" for twenty-four hours straight until, guess what, the rebels couldn't take it anymore." He continued: "Harsh warzone conditions. They do things like put your body up to your chest or head in water for hours upon hours. This goes on for weeks. It messes with your sensory information. You know how you feel after a night of no sleep or not enough sleep? Imagine weeks of this type of sensory offsetting. This lowers your defenses and makes you more open and susceptible to suggestion. There was this test some scientists did one time on mice or rats. They put them in a bucket of water with an upside-down cup two-thirds of the way underwater. They could climb the cup to get out of the water; the water wasn't high at all, but it was enough to be annoying for them. They would stand on this inverted cup and just chill out there, until they got sleepy. When they started to fall asleep, they would doze and fall into the water. They could fall asleep, but not hit the deep sleep. This test robbed them of REM sleep. What they found was without REM sleep they were driven bananas and their memory was horribly affected. Now imagine this on a large scale for humans," he finished, anticipating some backlash.

"C'est ridicule," Jean said.

"Shut up. I want to hear," Rosette replied.

NP kept going. He continued crossing things off the list. "First, you don't really know these new feelings. Then you seem to lose track of time. These brainy pests, they rise spy banter inside the binary gland. We're all, this everything, is all matrix-coded information, 1s and 0s. We just experience it holographically. These MK trainers start spy training inside the 1s-and-0s gland, aka the brain. There are four types of information sources. There is waveform energy, which you can see on brain scans, EEGs, heart EKGs, and so on and so forth. This is what information exists in, until observed by consciousness. The next level is electrical, which is irrelevant to this, but another is digital, which is the 1s and 0s that I was talking about. It's how computers are coded. The last level is holographic. It's how our brain takes the 1s and 0s and converts it third dimensionally or fourth density. The next step in programming would be something like this. You can be hooked up to a chair and forced to watch horrific images over and over again. Extreme visual trauma. It's the Ludovico technique, except it's used to trigger your subconscious instead of Pavlovian training of your conscious mind. Remember the scene in *Clockwork Orange* with the teardrops in the movie theater? No? It's okay if you don't; way before your time," he said.

"You're younger than us, dipshit," Hannah interjected.

"Whatever. So I'm basically talking about overloading the visual cortex after sensory deprivation. What's next on his list? Warzone conditions. When you're beat down, they hook you up to an IV so you are getting your fluids and make sure that your vitals are within systolic range. Then they torture you. Maybe they will rip your fingernails off one by one with pliers; maybe some electroshock therapy; who knows. I won't go on. Eventually, and this happens to everyone, you hit a point where your pain is so great that your threshold breaks and you pass out, except you can't physically go unconscious because there is a cocktail of drugs that prevent you from mentally turning off." NP paused a moment to catch his breath.

"How's that work exactly?" Rosette added.

"Let's put it like this. There are drugs that can put you to sleep instantly. Drugs that can put you in a medically induced coma. Drugs that can wake you up from both at the drop of a hat. So is it that outrageous to believe that there aren't drugs that can keep you conscious no matter what? Think about that for a minute. What happens is that either your mind just dies at its breaking point, or what usually happens to preserve your life because that's what we are all encoded to do—survive; it fractures to become another person to protect the original psyche. Only this new personality is a newborn with a blank slate. New and can be manipulated and trained." He continued: "Think about any movie you've seen about multiple-personality disorder or any TV show. It's always a stronger personality that comes out when the weaker one needs help. Think about multiple personalities like a bunch of Sims that don't know one other and that live in different rooms of the same house. You would be the main character but when one is needed, you would go into your room and another would come out of their room, do what has to be done either by visual or auditory triggers, then go back into the room. Then you come back out. You'd never know anything was different." NP waited for a response from anyone to make sure they were still following.

"You're saying you can do this procedure a bunch of times to the same person?" I said.

"And the personalities never meet one another. It's like in that movie *Identity*. Well, until the end when they all forced meet one another. I guess that's a bad example. Good movie, though," NP added.

"What would the point of this be, though? How would they use it?" I asked.

"Have you ever seen a hypnotist give a person a suggestion via auditory or visual cues?

Remember when one came to your middle school or high school? It's the same basic concept. Except that it's permanent. Again, the government uses them to kill people. Also, if they get caught, they would never know they had the information in their heads," he replied.

"Is there direct evidence of this occurring?" Hannah asked somewhat snidely.

"People always need their evidence. Unless someone comes up to you and says 'I'm a split personality sent here with orders to bend you over the barrel of this gun,' they won't believe it. How about I give you a derivative of what I'm talking about here. Lennon autographed a copy of *Double Fantasy* for Mark David Chapman six hours before he died. The ironic double fantasy was Chapman meeting and getting a signature and then coming back and killing Lennon. Chapman's father was a sergeant in the US Air Force; right there it gave him the access to MK military programming. Two, his father was physically abusive, which is an absolute bonus when trying to create another personality. It allows the test to disassociate easier," he finished. I was beginning to become a bit worried about why my best friend since childhood knew this much about reprograming a brain.

"Easier?" Hannah injected again.

"I mean, think about it. When you're being beaten and abused, after a while you start to accept it and, when it happens, you begin to picture yourself somewhere else. You fantasize about floating away, that it's not happening to you but to someone else. Rose, you're a psych grad student: isn't this textbook psychology for classifying things like borderline personality, bipolar, psychosis, D.I.D. M.P.D? The only difference is in MK programming, the pain and sensory distortion is never-ending and you literally split.

The point about Chapman is that he had all the markers. He shot Lennon, so what did he do? It was 1980. No cell phones, no cameras, none of this instant fame. He could have gotten away, or at least tried to. No, he sat there and read *The Catcher in the Rye*. Doesn't that seem a bit odd to you? I mean, think about it psychologically. People's end game to get caught usually would only be found if they were going after someone who killed someone close to them or to their dearly beloved. This was not the case. This wasn't a guy who killed his mother or brother. It was Lennon. All Lennon did was kill the Beatles when the industry pushed him too hard. What did Chapman do again? Get a signature, come back later, shoot him, then stand around? That's a pretty crappy end game. If I flip the script and this is, again, straight out of his letter. *S&M, Ladies, Entertainers & Politicians, Army of Pet,; Easter and Halloween.* This is the exact same thing, but the female version.

"Now you've got my attention!" Jean added.

"Shut up. Wait, I don't follow," Rose said.

"I wasn't one-hundred percent sure earlier, so I ran back and found a book on the origin of furry fetishes. These are people who are attracted to animals with human characteristics like, I dunno, Roxanne from *A Goofy Movie*," NP said. What was it with this guy and eighties and nineties references?

"Ha-ha. Really? You're attracted to animals with human features?" Hannah queried.

"Seriously, did you really just ask me that? Twist this around on itself, though. Aren't people trained to be attracted to humans with animal features? What animals do you think of for what did he say here in the letter? Easter and Halloween?

"Rabbit and black cat," Hannah said.

"Close. How about a BUNNY and KITTY which are incidentally also PET names for COUGARS. How many girls dress up like bunnies and sexy cats for Halloween? Why is the centerfold of the month called the *Playboy* Bunny?" NP asked us.

"Your elite gold-glove membership should be able to answer that for us," Rosette replied.

"Rose, can you by any chance walk to your car later in the dark alone?" he sneered.

"Ha-ha. I love you, too, Pierce," Rose said.

"This doesn't impress me," Jean replied.

"That might not, but maybe this will." I pulled out the watch from my pocket and showed everyone. I unscrewed the sidepiece, where you would normally set the time and date. I then plugged the watch into the computer. Jean's eyes bugged out of his head. He was with me at the White House when ironically the Secretary of Defense handed it over to me.

"Unbelievable. Wait a sec. Wait, did you use your computer at home?" NP asked.

"I didn't. I figured we could use yours," I replied.

"Excellent," he said. He went back to the board and looked it over. Crossed off *kept in time*. I was a little surprised at how put back Jean is being at this point but three hours ago I was in his boat, so I guess I couldn't complain. We plugged the watch drive in and right away a file popped up. I opened it. The first sentence: *Look very closely at my basic instructions before leaving Earth, little bro. The writing is in the sky.* After we both read the first document, NP looked at me and then at everyone. We knew we were onto something big…we just didn't know what.

CHAPTER 10

After going over this letter for another half-hour, Rose and I decided it was best to go speak to our old teacher, Mr. Rosibuild. Like NP, Rosibuild seemed to be dialed into all sorts of topics that would be helpful in uncovering what this letter was all about. We said our goodbyes as NP kept working in the library.

On the ride over to Interlock, I figured I'd see what else was on the watch. We were making progress but it wasn't fast enough. Luckily, Rosette kept her tablet on her at all times. I still couldn't get over this Bond nonsense. James, you are something else, man…were something else. Still need to get used to that. Just fought back an urge to jump out the window at the bar we'd just passed. Instead I plugged the drive in.

Day 1: James's thought of the day:

A Type-One civilization has harnessed its planetary power. They control earthquakes, the weather, volcanoes, anything planetary they control, that's type 1. A type 2 civilization is stellar. They've exhausted the power of a planet and they get their energy directly from their mother star. They use solar flares, the power of the sun to energize their huge machines.

—Michio Kaku (Theoretical Physicist. Referring to the Kardashev Scale)

Scientists have determined through completion of the genome project that humans are roughly 99.7 percent identical, DNA wise. Two penguins are more genetically different than you and I are. Whomever finds this, I want you to try this experiment. Write your name down. Write your two parents' names down above yours. Now you have four grandparents, eight great-grandparents, and you go on. Let's go back thirty-five generations. It roughly takes you back to the year 840 A.D. You will have 137 billion people.

The number of ancestors list reminds me of the story of the servant summoned by the Pharaoh. The Pharaoh was pleased with how the servant was doing and wanted to reward him. 'Serving you is all I desire, sir,' the servant insisted. 'No, I insist you ask for something, anything, you desire,' the Pharaoh said back. This went back and forth until the Pharaoh got mad and threatened punishment. After thinking long and hard, the servant, seeing a chessboard in front of him, said, 'On day one, I want one piece of rice; on the second I want two. Each day you will double the previous day's until this chessboard is complete. I will place a grain on each square representing each day completed.' The first day, the Pharaoh sent his finest servant and a parade with a golden pouch to deliver the grain. The amount grew exponentially and halfway through the board, there was no more grain in the land. The Pharaoh summoned the servant back in. 'Your highness, all I ever wanted to do was serve you,' replied the servant.

The servant, although now the wealthiest man in all the land, had retained his hubris. It was there that the Pharaoh learned not to question humility or assume that giving material gifts as tokens of appreciation were all that mattered. As for the servant, he continued to work for the Pharaoh, however he had taken all the rice and continued to feed all the poor and homeless until the day of his death.

The point of both these stories is that it's simple math; in fact, it's how cells divide in your body and mass-produce. The reason I stopped at this particular time frame is because roughly how many people it's been calculated that have ever lived on planet Earth. One hundred and forty billion people, that is. Even if we take the Bible literally, we need to still get to October 23, 4004 B.C.E. We're in a bit of a pickle here. There needs to be a way to bridge the gap and this is where the pedigree collapse comes in. The concept states that:

1) There is no other explanation other than a whole lot of incest. Sometimes, like in the case of the Kentucky Blue people, there are no branches on the family tree. Sometimes, like in the banking or royal families, it's to preserve money or "special genetics."
2) Based on our DNA, geneticists say that the farthest point one person can be on this planet from another is fiftieth cousins.
3) If your mom was from country x and your dad from country x as well, there's a twenty-percent chance they share a common ancestor within ten generations back.
4) So what does it all mean? Well, in a nutshell it means far enough back we are all related and all one and we should start to act like it. Let's explore different cognitive viewpoints.

How about from a *creationist*, then? Well, we all came from Adam and Eve. Technically Eve from Adam's rib and even more technically Adam was made from mud and dirt from the world God created.

How about from an *evolutionist*, then? Okay. Let's start with the Big Bang. Let alone the fact that all the material we are came from an infinitesimally dense singularity and nobody seems to want to explain where that singularity came from, but we'll let that slide. We all were one at one point.

How about the idea of *source energy*, then?

Hmmm. I'll try. If our souls are like crumbs off a cookie, the cookie being Source (God), whatever you want to call it, then we are all connected multi-dimensionally, and upon death it will be a vibrational change of frequency back to it.

Let's try one last one. *Aliens placing us here.* You would still have to account for the first humans and how we all came about. You don't just magically have a species poof, we're here. Or do you? If so, who created this first test group of people? Secondly, what about the first "spirit consciousness of DNA" that evolved this level of higher thinking. There is a big difference between what I am writing and a monkey who's fed up with people taking pictures of him and throwing his shit at them. Still, though, the point is that at some point things had to come back to a singularity in the sense of one source of point. Humans are so quick to think of the end of the world, things ending, but what they can't do is think about the beginning, or if there was something before a beginning.

—James

"You know, the Dalai Lama once said that if every eight-year-old was taught to meditate, than there would be peace on Earth in a generation," I said to Rose.

"Do you know what an EMT full of women is called?" Rose giggled.

"Oh God please not now Rose." I replied

"A clambulance!" Rose quipped, completely avoiding my comment.

"There's a gem," I replied.

"This reminds me of Pierce's 'You don't think about the things you've never thought about' sentence, no?" Rose said. "I mean, think about all the money they spend according to Pierce on fluoridating the water, chemtrails, tinkering with the food supply. It's got to be expensive. If the elite wanted a country of morons, wouldn't it be cheaper to just legalize incest?" she said.

"That would solve that problem for sure," I said.

This went on for a few minutes, Rose dropping gems and me trying not to laugh. This is a game we've always played where one person says the most ridiculous or offensive thing they can think of and the other has to be the deadpan serious one. I looked at my watch. Five p.m. Knowing Rosibuild, he'd be at the football bleachers with the debate team. As we pulled up to the parking lot by the football field, sure enough. Looked a little older, a little fatter than I remember; guess that makes sense, right? What debate coach carries around a whistle like a football coach? When he saw us, he nearly exploded.

"All right, all. You're dismissed for the day. Papers on Ben Franklin's autobiography from a philosophical point of view as applicable to the religious time frame due tomorrow. First draft, that is," Rosibuild said and waited for the last person to leave before he turned to address us. "Ha-ha! Well, you look a hell of a lot more sober than you did at the funeral," he said.

"I thought you didn't have it." I was referring to the fact that Rosibuild didn't have cable.

"I do have a television, but only for the DVDs I buy. You know I don't normally watch the news or any of that crap they put on there. I went to the bar to watch the speech. How you doin', boy? Rosette. My God. Look at you, girl. You two finally turned it into something? I always had a feeling about it." He puffed.

"No, no, just really good friends still. Graham's actually engaged," Rosette said.

"Almost engaged." I tried to end this conversation as quickly as possible. There was this one party a few years ago when Rose and I got so drunk, well, let's just say too drunk and it didn't work out. This was long before I met Hannah. Still, though. "I see you're still running them into the ground like you did with us," I said.

"I've evolved since your days here at Interlock. I've developed a new method to forge young minds into the future of this world since your black-and-white silent film days here. Care to hear?"

"Sure," Rose jumped in.

"Each one of them writes a topic on a piece of paper. Politics, abortion, et cetera. Each week we pick one of them. I split a few of them up into two groups based on their beliefs; I let them pick. Then they work until Wednesday afternoon drafting their arguments. Then right before the end of class Wednesday, I pull them aside; the small teams that are up for debate that is, and I make them switch sides completely. They have one day to put together and argue the opposite."

"That seems a bit cruel, no?" Rose asked.

"This is how you develop critical thinkers, darling. The problem with most people is they are just too stuck in their own way. They only seek out other likeminded thinkers once they have developed their own ideas. How the hell do you break ground with a stubborn S.O.B. at that point?" he asked.

"I see your point," I replied.

"Of course you do. You always were one of my brightest. Still hang around with that tweaky fellow with the crazy ideas?"

"Of course. Look, I hate to cut this nostalgia short but is there somewhere we can talk?" I pressed.

"We are talking, ain't we?" he said.

"Look, my brother left me something before he died. The President asked me if he sent me any writing and I didn't tell her at the time. I thought it was a letter, but it looks like a cryptocode," I said.

"Get out of here."

"It's true," Rosette jumped in. Normally, I would have said this was crazy, but listen to who it's coming from. He had a watch that you plug into your computer like a flash drive with this writing and all this information on it," she finished.

"All right. Let's head back to my house; it's five minutes away from here," he said.

"You sure?" I replied.

"These computers here have these plugins in back that are basically backup directories. It looks like a flash drive you plug into the computer, but I looked up the company. It saves everything that you are doing and backs it up to a general server. This probably isn't the kind of thing you want getting out, right?" he asked.

As we were waiting in the car in front of the school, I plugged the watch back in. What else you got, James?

Day 2: Thought of the day

Maybe it's just me but I'm always brought back to this Native American quote any time I hear anything. "When the Last Tree Is Cut Down, the Last Fish Eaten, and the Last Stream Poisoned, Only then Will We Realize that You Cannot Eat Money." Just know I'm not suicidal. Not now, not ever—I love and enjoy life. Despite all the above, I still have faith in people.

—James

I rolled the window down for some air. What did I just read? I went back to it to make sure I saw what I saw. *I'm not suicidal, period. Not now, not ever – I love and enjoy life.* I knew it all along. There's no way he would have killed himself. Twice the President had lied to me. I felt the rage build up and those familiar feelings of wanting to drown them out, but this time I felt stronger feelings from the pit of my stomach wanting to get to the bottom of this. I was going to figure this out and one thing was for certain: when I figured it out, I was going to confront her on it. I just kept picturing the skeleton CPR and remembering that I needed to think of every angle. This was the President we were talking about. What did my brother know that they had to silence him for?

"Remember when searching for the truth, that rat poison is 99% food and only 1% cyanide. It's the only way to draw the rat in. The poison blends in with what it was looking for not realizing what has just happened until its' too late."

—Anonymous

CHAPTER 11

I sat in my thoughts for a minute and started to float away when I snapped back to the situation at hand. I remember something my brother always used to tell me when I was growing up. He'd say that if you live in the past, you will always be depressed because you can't reclaim it; if you live in the future, you will always be anxious looking at how much you have to do; the only thing you can do is live in the now because that is really the only time that exists. All calendars are different, clocks are different, time zones are different. If you just sit inside your skin and think for a minute, now is the only real time. Smart guy. Then I found out from NP he was quoting Buddha. Who was this guy I was related to?

"Jean. It's me. Look, we just got to my old history teacher, Mr Rosibuild's, house. We're going over the letter and some information. I don't know if you ended up meeting back up with Hannah and NP, but just wanted to fill you in. I'll give you a call when I'm back in town, okay?" I left the voicemail and turned the knob on his front door. Walking into Mr. Rosibuild's house, I noticed that it looks like nothing had been touched since his wife had passed away years before. Everything was exactly where it had been left. I've heard of enshrining someone, but this was a catacomb.

"Snap back into it, Newsdon, I don't have much time here," he said to me as I was glazing down his house. "I've looked over this letter. He mentioned the precession of the equinox. You do know what that is, right?"

"Vaguely," I replied

"It's a slow shift, like spinning a top. It happens every 26,000 years. Now, take a pen and paper; I'm going to teach you something. You break this down by the zodiac," he said.

"As in the astrology signs?" I played a bit dumb remembering how NP had already revolved this around the zodiac. Things were trying to line up; I just couldn't see where yet.

"Every seventy-two years, the Earth tilts one degree. Non-coincidentally, seventy-two years is roughly the average lifespan of a man and a woman, if you average them. Usually women outlive the men…usually." He trailed off as memories of his wife must have flooded back.

"I see all these pictures of Mrs. Rosibuild around. She seemed like she was such a great—"

Rosette began before being cut off.

"Thank you, Rose, but never mind that now. Every seventy-two years it tilts one degree. Each zodiac sign is thirty degrees of the sky. Multiply them together, you get 2,160 years. Now, you take that and multiply it by the twelve signs and you get 25,920 or the 26,000 I was talking about," he said.

"That's incredible," I said, overacting.

"Well, thank you, but it's just simple math, boy," Rosibuild said, sensing that I had already heard about the zodiac prior to our current conversation. I guess I should jump in now.

"No. I mean, look in the first part of the letter; he encoded all these zodiac symbols. NP, sorry, Mr. Pierce, as you called him, has this theory that the first should be Aquarius and the last Leo, how James had brought it up in his letter. Since the rest are jumbled, it's the only substantial outlier," I said.

"Precession means that the signs go backward in relation to the equinox. It would actually be in reverse then. Starting with Leo and then ending with Aquarius. I just told you how long it was, but I never told you when it was. You're familiar with December 21, 2012. The Mayan date?" he asked.

"Yeah, that was supposed to be the end of the world…the end of times," Rosette said.

"The end of my ass! This wasn't no end of times. It was the end of a time. The end of

Pisces…" He trailed off so I could complete the thought.

"And the beginning of the Age of Aquarius," I finished.

"Exactly. Now, look. Here's another important part I have to show you and then I have to let you go because an old man needs to get his nap on before he starts grading quizzes. He said he was a rapper. Boy, the day that happens I'll try that coat parachute off the school clock tower myself," he said.

Rosibuild was always obsessed with this guy, Franz Reichelt, who died in 1912 when he jumped off the bridge of the Eiffel Tower with an invention he called a coat parachute, which was exactly that: a coat that looked like a parachute. Didn't work out quite like Superman. The press was there and filmed the whole thing. The Eiffel Tower wasn't a full Masonic Triangle yet, as NP likes to say. It's Darwin's idea in action. Or who I thought was Darwin. I don't know what to think anymore.

"Flo Rida, no, Flo Ride. I thought it was some corny pun at first. But then in the next sentence he talks about antidepressants and his heart and I realized he was talking about fluoride."

"Talking about what now? You mean the stuff they put in toothpaste? Yeah, NP won't let me use the fluoridated stuff anymore. Says it calcifies your pineal and makes you think all fuzzylike," I said.

"It does more than that. It makes you docile. If fluoride is so good for you, why does it say to call the poison control center if you swallow some? What's more is that most antidepressants contain fluoride—they're just not labeled."

"Is that the real reason people take them and become calm?" Rose asked.

"That's why people take them and I can light them on fire and they wouldn't piss on themselves to put it out. Okay, seriously, one last thing and then you really need to go. There's something I've been working on for a while; give me a minute and let me go grab it," he said as he scuffled off up his flight of stairs and pulled down the lever to the stairs to his attic. I couldn't possibly imagine what he would need from up there. After a brief moment, he emerged from the darkness with a small book.

"That was the most exercise I've gotten all week. All right. What is the number-one killer in America today?" he asked me.

"Heart disease."

"People are not aware that cholesterol is supported by inflammation, which causes plaque buildup, which is the major cause of most strokes and heart attacks. Instead of curing them with the vaccines that we have, or even treating properly the first time, they do procedures like balloon angioplasties, which smash the plaque against the artery and open the highway from a single lane to two. Problem is eventually traffic builds up again and this just delays the inevitable. Eventually a bypass surgery will have to happen. This guarantees maximum dollar extraction from said patient. Two juicy heart procedures. You've heard of a double, triple, quadruple, bypass? That depends on how many traffic lanes they need to close off. Here's the thing, though. When people die, they do autopsies. They cut out these arteries and squeeze all this shit out of them. Like that old smoking commercial years back, remember? Well, they test this junk. More than a decent amount of it is hydrocarbon buildup and not just fats. What are most pharmaceuticals made of?" he said.

"Jesus," I said.

"Not quite, but exactly. Hydrocarbons. All these medications that people take on a daily basis leave a trail on the highway. The same goes for the cancer industry. Before the polio vaccine in the fifties, cancer wasn't on a top-ten list of deaths. Never mind the fact that by the time they rolled out the polio vaccine, deaths were already on their way down. Secretly they found that this virus, the SV 40 virus, carried over from monkeys to humans. When ninety million people were inoculated with the polio vaccine, it transferred the SV 40. Consequently, the cancer population shot up from not on the list at all in the 1940s to the number-two killer since the 1950s and has been number two ever since."

"Why would monkeys have anything to do with it?" Rose asked.

"Because when you're trying to cure a virus or a disease, it's not polite to just stick humans with a cure without testing it on expendables such as animals. I've had a lot of time on my hands to do some reading since my wife passed. One last thing, Mr. Newsdon," he said.

"What's that?" I asked.

"Before you go, I just wanted to tell you how proud I am that your brother found Christ before he died."

"What do you mean?" I said.

"I mean, look at all the times he mentioned it?" he said as he jumped all over the letter. "Presbyterians, keep a close eye on the priests, everyone needs a messiah. Run to St. Peters Church. Continue until the day star rises in your heart. That which sustains us? Talking about our Lord Jesus. Good for him. I urge you to turn to Him as well and find your answers."

"Thanks Mr. R. Always great seeing you. I still remember that speech you gave at graduation." I didn't want to go into the fact that I was going to parrot it at my brother's funeral, until I found out it was a suicide.

"Well, they say if you can touch one kid in that special way. Damn, don't read into that sentence, boy. Now go on," he said as he shut the door.

As we left, I started thinking back to what

Rosibuild just said; it sounded good on paper, but a few things were off. We weren't Presbyterians; we were Roman Catholics and the church across the street was St. Thomas and not St. Peters. Normally I would have let that slide but words are not an accident, right? We had to convene in the morning. I needed some sleep and to compartmentalize.

"You spending the night, Rose?" I asked.

"I practically live there, remember?" she replied.

As we pulled into our driveway, little did we know a call was being made from inside the Rosibuild residence.

"How's it going? Long time. No, it's all good over here. I just had a lovely chance encounter with some old friends. No, former students, from the TV the other day during the military funeral. The one, she, yeah, the woozy kid. Uh-huh. Nothing yet, but they're well on their way. I didn't give them much, just something they could look up online if they wanted to, and some medical stuff to fill that Newsdon boy's head. I know, but believe me, nobody thought it would come to this; this was the worst-case scenario. He has a letter from his brother. I'm not sure it wasn't handwritten. No, I didn't get a copy of it; are you crazy? No, it seems like that quirky kid with the high IQ; the one he's always with who seems to be running the show. No, I don't think they have anything of substance yet, but there's definitely information coded in the letter. Because I saw it with my own eyes. Nope, this is textbook. I understand. Talk to you soon."

CHAPTER 12

"I need to know everywhere that Newsdon and Pierce kid have been in the last three months, goddammit." Lilac fumed as she puffed furiously on her fake cigarette. Those things don't even taste like real cigarettes or give the nicotine buzz that would calm her down right then. But after her husband got sick, she made a promise to him that she would never smoke again. Just because he was gone didn't mean she was going to break a promise to him. The night before, as she was enjoying her Prosecco, kind of, she was just getting used to the idea that maybe there was nothing going on and her paranoia was getting the best of her. That call from the disgraced priest changed everything in a heartbeat. She could feel herself losing control of this situation and she was not one who liked to lose control of anything. "I meant yesterday!" Lilac fumed once more.

"Lilly, you really need to relax. You're going to burst a blood vessel. What is getting all wound up right this minute going to accomplish that you can't if you just calm down."

Jake always knew exactly what to say to her.

Again, she couldn't understand how that trait could have been transferred from her husband to another man.

"They'll find your information and then we'll take it from there; that's the best we can do," he said.

"The best we can do is not enough. Right now there is a small house of semi-brilliant minds looking over a letter that James somehow managed to sneak past our infinite security and get to his brother. A letter that we still don't know anything about. How do you think this makes us look?" Lilac questioned.

"Do you really want me to answer that? I'm not going to," Jake replied. "Lilly, did you have James on a top-secret assignment?" Jake asked.

"Of course. They all were," she replied, hoping it would end there.

"That's not what I meant and you know it. This kid's test scores are through the roof; he's built like a ton of bricks and speaks three languages. I'm going to ask again… please be honest with me. Was there anything that he was getting into that we don't know about?"

"Jake, you know if he was, I would have consulted you by now," Lilac replied. Of course it was a lie that went under the radar of the trusting Jake. There was so much information that he was unaware of in all avenues of her work. Secret clearance all the way to the top. "What I can't wrap my head around was why did it show up now? Why not a few months ago. Why are we dealing with this now that he's dead?" the President wondered out loud.

"I don't know, but there has to be a logical explanation for all of this. To the letter; to the writing in the letter. Unfortunately, until we know how he got the letter or if there are any copies, we can't do anything. We can't expose ourselves to them just yet. God knows what they would do if they knew we know even just what we know now," Jake finished.

"You're right," the President said. "Should we tap their house and computers?"

"Already done. It doesn't seem like they're ones for computers or house lines lately," Jake replied.

"Well, what about their cell phones? Any chatter on it?"

"Unfortunately, no. Whatever they're doing and however they're doing it, they're avoiding all the usual suspects," Jake replied.

"Madam President, you're going to want to see this," Roger interrupted.

He led her into the conference room and on the projector was a picture of James's passport from his undercover North Africa days.

"It seems that our boy took a flight to Hamburg and spent the night, paid the hotel in cash. Anyway, he gets on a train to Dusseldorf the next morning using one of his other passports which we gave to him when he was in the Baltics. The trail goes cold there. I mean, there is no longer anything that ties him there. Then magically four days later he shows up here in Cologne at a café, takes a train back to Berlin, where he flies back."

"Roger, I don't have to tell you how unacceptable it is that the trail ends. I need to know what his next move was. Flag all his credit cards, passports, everything," Lilac said.

"Already done, Madam President. It looks like he was using cash for this entire trip. Nothing came up."

"Where does a Marine come up with that kind of cash to blow?" she fumed.

"Nothing yet, but believe me we're still looking into it. What do you want to do with that priest?" Roger asked.

"Nothing yet. Keep him close by, though. I've got a bad feeling about this," she said.

Lilac started walking back toward the Vermeil Room. For some reason, she always found that room nicer to relax in than the Lincoln or Roosevelt Room. Even her own bedroom as of late was getting a bit stuffy. They should rename it the wine-and-shitty TV room, Lilac joked to herself. Then this feeling in the pit of her stomach started churning and she had to sit down. For a split second it was as if she had forgotten all that had happened the previous month. There was no way this letter could have anything to do with it. Could it?

"Has any great change on your planet ever been created by anyone who wasn't crazy? Who didn't go against the grain of the norm? So why not join the club and be crazy? It's a nice club to be in. Then you will simply gravitate to and attract to you people of the same kind of crazy and then when you are in a community of people who are the same kind of crazy, you won't be crazy. You'll be normal."
—Bashar

CHAPTER 13

"I think he's dead," Rosette said.

"Well, c'mon, team. Wake 'em up. Ain't nobody got time for that. We've got a lot to do here," NP replied. They were talking about me. Seems that since my brother's death, I had a newfound respect for sleep. I was jolted out of a bizarre dream by Rose jumping on the couch; well, technically, on me on the couch. The President was giving a speech on the Hill and I was trying to confront her about my brother, but I just couldn't get to her; there was a swarm of supporters just tossing admiration her way. Now why would I have that dream?

"How long was I out?" I asked.

"About ten hours," Hannah said. Apparently they thought it was best to let a med student sleep everything off, but enough was enough already.

"I filled them in while you were out. Get up.

Here. Slurpee. Ow, ow," she said.

"What's wrong?" I replied, startled.

"Brain freeze!" she shrieked.

"Put your tongue on the roof of your mouth and press hard. It'll deflect the sensation." I yawned. After a minute, her face broke into a big smile.

"How did you do that?" she said.

"Brain freeze is caused by blood flow to the anterior cerebral artery. As soon as it's constricted, it wears off and the pain goes away. NP, I need to tell you something before I forget," I said.

"Just setting the boards up," he replied while working furiously.

"I was thinking about this at the house. The things that we need the most—e-mail, food, travel—they are all named after water," I said.

"For once, you've lost me."

"Well, I mean, Rosette's got a Mizu; I've got a Shui 3.0. That's water in Japanese and Chinese. So, I get it: Americans make pieces of shit technology and cars. Fine. But I have a Hydragua e-mail like most of America at this point. Also, I was thinking. Rosibuild brought up my brother being religious out of nowhere. Got me thinking about Jesus and then the Jesus fish popped into my head. Why the fish? Does that make any sense? I mean, in the Bible Jesus talks about fish a lot, I've heard, but isn't it ironic," I finished as NP looked at the board for a few minutes then spun around and looked at us like he was about to turn into the Tasmanian Devil. I'm seriously going to need to invest in an AED between all these people. If Doc Brown from *Back to the Future* did lines of espresso and grated cayenne peppers, you know what, never mind. I wouldn't have changed him for the world because maybe his brain wouldn't work the same or something. He plugged his borrowed-from-work laptop into the printer and started pounding away. After about fifteen minutes, he came out with this chart. As well as a few additional documents.

LEO 10948BC-8788BC
CANCER 8788BC- 6628BC
GEMINI 6628BC-4468BC
TAURUS 4468BC-2308BC
ARIES2308BC-148BC
PISCES 148BC-DEC 21, 2012 AD
AQUARIUS DEC 22, 2012AD- 4172AD

He then went to the board and under Aquarius wrote everything I brought up. Under Pisces, he wrote *Jesus*. "We know that all calendars are different, so we need a jump-off point. I'm comfortable stealing Gestasbuild's idea about the Mayan end of Pisces, so we can date stamp this. Mayan end date of Dec 21, 2012," he said.

"Of course. Also, yes, this teacher you keep talking about sounds very much like a jester indeed," Jean said.

This reference went well above Jean's ever-so-slight language barrier, but I knew he was referring to Gestas, the man crucified to the left of Christ who kept insisting that he could save himself. He was the ultimate thief, a trait that NP had considered Rosibuild having for most of his life.

"Look at the time frame of the Old Testament. It's right before Pisces because remember it's the precession of the equinox, so we're going backward in the zodiac. Well, right before the Christians in the Pisces timeframe were the Jews; during Aries, the ram. If we're using the Bible itself as an encoded book and follow this train of thought, it blows this entire thing wide open. But what's right before Aries? It's Taurus. This was the time period during which the Egyptians were large and in charge. The Jews were the slaves. Their homeland was to be Israel, which is directly influenced by the Egyptians, as it stands for Isis, Ra, El. Exodus takes place roughly 1,500 years B.C.E., which is during Aries. You're talking about Moses climbing Mount Sinai to receive the Ten Commandments and he comes down and sees what?"

"People worshipping a golden calf," Hannah said.

"A calf is what exactly? The sun is what color? He sees a golden bull. He sees the sun coming up against the Taurus sky. Why does he get so mad and break the Commandments? Because they were worshipping the time period they'd just escaped from. All those years of slavery in Taurus. Now it is Aries and they are free. Which is why nowadays during the holidays the Jews will blow the ram's horn up to the sky. The Ram being Aries." He continued: "So either this is what the story is alluding to, or these poor wandering Jews walked around in the desert for forty years with nothing, yet had enough gold to weld the largest gold animal in the world? Is that the first thing you would do when your leader says, 'Be right back; going into the mouth of a volcano to get the Commandments from God for you. I know you're tired and hungry and probably delusional and thirsty, but just hang out for a while.' Build a giant gold calf?" He paused for a moment to collect his thoughts as he pointed to a hieroglyphic printout. "What do you see here? Bulls, rams, fish, lions? Or maybe Taurus, Aries, Pisces, Leo. What are these little things here? Scarabs? Remember our talk earlier about how they represent the same as crabs?

"Where are we going with this?" I asked.

"Remember that movie that came out a few years ago about how the story of Christ was just a parroted story and that there were plenty of previous 'gods' that were born on December 25 that were born of a virgin mother, that fought something, were killed, and then resurrected?"

"Yeah, so? It's the same story ripped from previous stories; what's the point?" I asked.

"But what if it's not 'ripped from previous stories?' What if it's the *only* story that keeps trying to be taught to civilization after civilization?" With that, he propped up this diagram that I was going to have to get very familiar with.

"We're still going backward, actually. 'Remember before that happened how I buried you up to your head in the sandbox. I show people the photo but it's stupid because you were facing the wrong way. Looking at that picture of the lion helps me keep my perspective in the right direction,'" He said, quoting my brother's letter.

With that, he pulled this out:

"This is what the Sphinx looked like a generation after Napoleon made his way across Europe," NP started before being interrupted.

"Sacrilege! There were no cameras back then," Jean said.

"You got me there, but Louis Daguerre invented a method of stop-motion capture called the daguerreotype. It was photography before photography. His first 'selfie' was taken in 1839. Can you just roll with the idea that with thousands of years of sandstorms, the Sphinx was buried and we're lucky we found anything at all? So anyway, they dug it up. Here is what it looks like now. You see the soft striation marks right on its backside? This is made from water, not wind or sand erosion.

Now it's a desert. I mean, I know it snowed there in December four years ago, but still—God, this has to be what he's talking about," he finished.

"What exactly?" I replied.

"Your costume wasn't ripped apart by ice or ripped apart at all. The last time there was any form of water or ice in the area by the lion, aka Sphinx, was the end of the ice age, circa 10,000 B.C.E. This is when the ice age officially ended and it started to finally melt," he said.

"Are you seriously trying to make the argument that the Sphinx was build 12,000 years ago?"

"If you follow the zodiac, it makes sense." With that, he referred to the dates of the signs chart he'd just provided: **LEO 10948BC-8788BC.** "If you notice where the Sphinx is facing, it would have been directly facing constellation Leo around 10,000 B.C.E.

The dates line up. Also, have you heard of Orion's Belt?" With that, he pulled this one out:

"The great pyramids line up perfectly with Orion's Belt, which is located in the Gemini and Taurus border." With that, he brought this chart back out, but added to it:

LEO 10948BC-8788BC Sphinx/Egyptians
CANCER 8788BC- 6628BC Egyptians
GEMINI 6628BC-4468BC
Pyramids/Orion/Egyptians
TAURUS 4468BC-2308BC
Pyramids/Orion/Egyptians/Golden Calf/Jews
ARIES2308BC-148BC Rams Horn/Jews
PISCES 148BC-DEC 21, 2012 AD
(Romans/Jews/Christ/Christians)

"What I'm saying, what I think your brother was getting to, is that Bible literalists believe the world is 6,000 years old and most Egyptologists believe roughly the same. But that's only because they're taking the Old and New Testaments literally. They are one and the same, talking about the Sun and the stars in different, hidden ways.

"It's not just the New Testament that hides the story of the zodiac and all the stars. Job 38:32: 'Can you lead forth the Mazzaroth?' The Mazzaroth is the zodiac. Mazzaroth over time becomes the Mazalot, which survives in Judaism today; mazel tov is 'good luck' or 'good fortune from the stars.' Now, here's what I'm getting at. The Lord's challenge to Job? I was flipping through it a little while ago and it's just littered with references to the stars. We can start with the obvious first one: 'Can you bind the chains of the Pleiades? Can you loosen Orion's Belt?' 'Can you bring forth the constellations in their seasons or lead out the bear with its cubs? The constellations are the zodiac above; the bear and its cubs are Ursa Major, the Great Bear, and Ursa Minor, part of the Big Dipper. 'Who can tip over the water jars of the heavens?' Aquarius. 'Do you hunt the prey for the lioness and satisfy the hunger of the lions?' Leo. 'Who provides food for the raven?' The constellation Corvus, which means raven and was bordering on Virgo. 'Do you watch when the doe bears her fawn?' Mriga, meaning deer, is located in Orion. Should I keep going? Okay, then. 'Who let the wild donkey go free?' Asellus Borealis means donkey and is located in Cancer. 'Will the wild ox consent to serve you?' That's simple, it's Taurus, one of the twelve zodiac signs. 'The wings of the ostrich flap joyfully.' Lambda Aquilae or Al Thalimain, which means 'two ostriches' in Arabic. 'Do you give the horse its strength?' 'It laughs at fear, afraid of nothing; it does not shy away from the sword, the quiver rattles against its side, along with the flashing spear and lance.' Sagittarius with the bow and arrow. 'Does the eagle soar at your command and build its nest on high?' Aquila is the Latin name for eagle and is a constellation a few degrees above the celestial equator. 'Can you pull in Leviathan with a fishhook?' The great fish Pisces." He stopped.

"If you use the zodiac and the stars, you'll find countless expressions of them in the Bible. The

Jesus fish is just symbolically referencing the astrological time it took place in, Pisces. In John, once Jesus has been resurrected, he's walking along the beach and he sees his disciples fishing. They can't catch anything. He tells them to throw the net to the other side of the boat. They end up reeling in 153 fish. Well, the Vesica PISCES (Pisces) has a ratio of 265/153; 153 is its denominator.

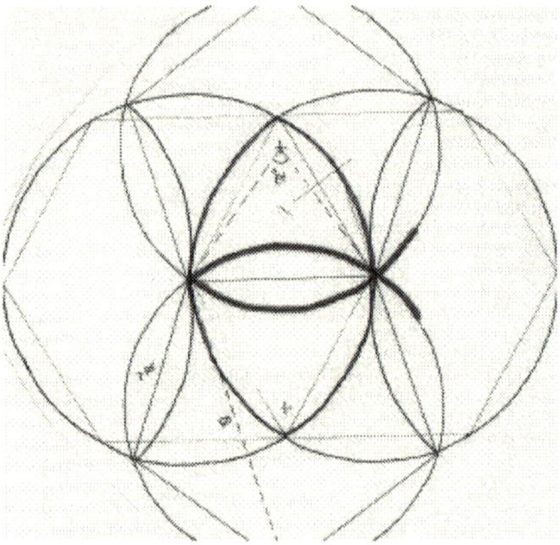

Let me go on: 'Spring is Aries, when the Jews hold the Passover or when the Sun passes over the equator on the 14th of Nisan. It's right in the middle of Aries every year. In Christ's literal manifestation, the Resurrection of Easter is in the same time period and this is where 'God's son/sun' starts its ascent to heaven. So you have the Passing Over and the Resurrection at the same time. Two phrases, one meaning. Summer would be Cancer/Leo as the ruling planet of Leo is in fact the Sun. This is the kingdom of heaven, when the Sun is in the summer months. Fall, which is Libra, is where the Sun is judged by the man with the scales before it's betrayed in Scorpio. By judged and betrayed, it is because it starts to get cold around there, as if the Sun is dying. This is all about Sun worship. Why is Scorpio a scorpion? I mean, why that specific animal? Well, first of all, if you look up at the night sky, it's the most beautiful constellation there is out there. It literally looks like a scorpion. But more importantly, back in ancient times when a scorpion would bite you, it would leave two marks in your skin that looked like lips. Have you heard of the 'kiss of death' before? That's where it comes from. It looks like a kiss, but it's full of poison—there's the betrayal. It's why Judas identified Jesus with a kiss, instead of pointing or so on and so forth. The sun is judged in Scorpio, whereas in Sagittarius, the bow and arrow inflicts further punishment on God's Sun before it dies, only to be reborn again in a new year, to continue this cycle," he said.

"This feels like a stretch," I said, speaking for everyone in the room, as one by one I put the zodiac signs into NP's computer that he was using, starting with Leo and going backward in the precession of signs. With each search, my heart sank deeper into my stomach while everyone's, especially NP's, eyes got wider.

Lion/Leo

2 Timothy: 4:17; 1 Peter: 5:8; Revelations: 4:7; 5:5; 9:8; 10:3; 13:2; Genesis: 49:9; Numbers: 23:24; 24:9; Deuteronomy; 33:20; 33:22; Judges: 14:5-6; 14:8-9; 14:18; 1 Samuel: 17:34; 17:36-37; 2 Samuel: 17:10; 23:20; 1 Kings: 10:19-20; 13:24-26; 13:28; 20:36; 1 Chronicles: 11:22; 12:8; 28:17; 2 Chronicles: 9:18-19; Job: 4:10-11; 10:16; 28:8; 38:39; Psalm 7:2; 10:9; 17:12; 22:13; 22:16; 22:21; 38:8; 91:13; 19:12; 20:2; 22:13; 26:13; 28:1; 28:15; 30:30; Ecclesiastes: 9:4; Isaiah: 5:29; 11:6-7; 15:9; 21:8; 30:6; 31:4; 35:9; 38:13; 65:25; Jeremiah: 2:30; 4:7; 5:6; 12:8; 25:30; 25:38; 49:19; 50:44; 51:38; Lamentations: 3:10; Ezekiel; 1:10; 10:14; 19:3; 19:5; 19:6; 19:2; 22:25; 32:2; 41:19; Daniel: 7:4 Hosea: 9:13; 11:10; 13:7; 13:8 Joel: 1:6; Amos: 1:2; 3:4; 3:8; 3:12; 5:19; Micah: 5:8 Nahum 2:11-12

Cancer (as spreading disease)

Proverbs: 12:4; 14:30 2 Timothy 2:17;

Cancer (as beetle)

Exodus: 8:21; 8:22; 8:24; 8:29; 8:31; Leviticus: 11:22; Psalm: 78:45; 105:31

Twins/Gemini

Acts: 28:11; Romans: 9:10-11; Genesis: 25:21; 25:24; 25:26; 38:27; Exodus: 36:29; Song of Solomon: 4:2; 4:5; 6:6; 7:3;

Bull/Taurus

Deuteronomy—18:3; 33:17; Leviticus—1:5; 4-12; 4:3-5; 4:7-8; 4:11; 4:14-17; 4:20-21; 8:2; 8:14-15; 8:17; 9:2; 16:14-15; 16:18; 16:27; 16:3; 16:6; 16:11, 22:23; 23:18; Numbers—7:21; 7:27; 7:39; 7:45; 7:15; 7:51; 7:57; 7:75; 7:63; 7:69; 7:81; 8:8; 15:8-9; 15:11; 15:24; 23:14; 23:2; 23:4; 23:30; 28:12; 28:14; 29:2-3; 29:36-37; 29:8; 29:9; Exodus—21:28-29; 21:31-32; 21:35; 21:36; 29:1; 29:3; 29:10-11; 29:12; 29:14; 29:36; 2 Chronicles 13:9; Job—21:10; 1 Samuel 1:24-25; 2 Samuel 6:13; Ezekiel-- 43:19; 43:21; 43:22-23; 43:25; 45:18; 45:22; 45:24; 46:6-7; 46:11; Kings—18:23; 18:26; 18:33; Psalms—50:9; 69:31; 106:20; Isaiah—34:7; 66:3;
Judges—6:25-26; 6:28;

Aries/Ram

Genesis: 15:9; 22:13; 30:41; 31:38; Exodus: 19:13; 19:16; 19:19; 20:18; 25:5; 26:14; 29:17; 29:15; 29:16; 29:18-20; 29:22, 29:26; 29:27; 29:31-32; 29:34; 35:7; 35:23; 36:19; 39:34; Leviticus: 4:35; 5:15; 5:18; 5:16; 6:6; 8:18; 8:19-24; 8:29; 9:2; 9:4; 9:18-19; 16:3; 16:5, 19:21-22; 22:19; 25:9; Numbers 5:8; 6:14; 6:17; 6:19; 6:20; 7:15; 7:21; 7:27; 7:33; 7:39; 7:45; 7:51; 7:57; 7:63; 7:69; 7:75; 7:81; 15:6; 15:11-12; 23:2; 23:4; 23:14; 23:30; 28:11-12; 28:14; 28:19-20; 28:27-28; 29:2-3; 29:8-9; 29:14; 29:36-37; Joshua: 6:4-6 (talks about the ram's horn); Judges: 6:34; 7:16; Ruth: 4:19 1 Samuel 13:3; 14:34; 17:34 Matthew 1:3-4; Luke 3:33;

Pisces/Fish

Genesis: 1:20; 1:22; 1:26; 1:28; 9:2; Exodus: 7:18; 7:21 Numbers: 11:5; 11:22; Deuteronomy: 4:18; 1 Samuel: 5:4 1 Kings: 4:33 2 Chronicles 33:14 Nehemiah: 3:3; 12:39; 13:16 Job: 12:8; 41:1; 41:7; Psalm: 8:8; 105:29; Ecclesiastes: 9:12; Song of Solomon 7:4; Isaiah 19:8; 19:10; 50:2; Jeremiah: 16:16; Ezekiel 29:4-5; 38:20; 47:9-10 Hosea: 4:3 Amos: 4:2 Jonah: 1:17: 2:1; 2:10; Habakkuk: 1:14; Zephaniah: 1:3; 1:10 Matthew: 4:19; 7:10; 12:40; 13:47; 13:48; 14:17; 14:19; 15:34; 15:36; 17:27; Mark: 1:17; 6:38; 6:41; 6:43; Luke: 5:4; 5:6-7, 5:9-10; 9:13; 9:16; 11:11; 24:42; John: 6:9; 6:11; 21:3; 21:5-6; 21:8-11; 21:13; Acts: 9:18 1 Corinthians: 15:39 James: 3:7

Aquarius/Man with Pitcher

(Water in a jar/pot)

Mark: 14:13; Luke: 22:10; John: 2:6; 4:28; Genesis: 24:14-17; 24:20; 24:43; 24:25; 24:46; Numbers: 5:17-18; 19:17

Capricorn/Goat

Luke 15:29; Hebrews 11:37; Revelation 6:12; Genesis 15:9; 27:16; 30:32-33; 37:31; 38:17; 38:20; 38:23; Exodus 12:3; 12:5-6; 12:21; 13:13; 23:19; 25:4; 26:7; 34:20; 34:26; 35:6; 35:23; 35:26; 36:14; Leviticus 1:10; 3:12; 3:13; 4:23-4; 4:26; 4:28; 4:31; 5:6-7; 7:23; 9:3; 9:15; 10:16; 10:18; 12:8; 16:8-10; 16:15; 16:18; 16:20-21; 16:26; 16:27; 17:3; 17:7; 22:19; 22:27; 23:19; 27:26; Numbers 7:16; 7:22; 7:28; 7:34; 7:30; 7:46; 7:52; 7:58; 7:64; 7:70; 7:76;

7:82; 15:5; 15:11; 15:24; 15:27; 18:17; 28:15; 28:22; 28:29-30; 29:5; 29:11; 29:16; 29:19; 29:22; 29:25; 29:31; 29:28: 29:34; 29:38; 31:20; 14:4-5; 14:21; 18:3; 22:1; Judges 6:19; 13:15; 13:19; 14:6; 15:1; 1 Samuel 16:20

Sagittarius/Archer, Bow, and Arrow
Genesis 21:16; 21:20; 2 Samuel 1:22; 22:35; 1 Samuel 20:36; 1 Kings 22:34;
2 Kings 9:24; 2 Chronicles 18:33; Job 20:24; 39:23; 41:28; Psalm 11:2; 18:34; 46:9; 58:7; 64:3; Isaiah 7:24; 22:3; Proverbs 6:5; 26:10; Jeremiah 4:29; 6:23; 50:14; 51:3; Lamentations 2:4; 3:12; Zechariah 9:13; Amos 2:15

Scorpio/Scorpion
Luke 10:19; 11:12: 2 Chronicles 10:11; 10:14; 1 Kings 12:11; 12:14; Ezekiel 2:6; Judges 1:36: Joshua 15:3; Number 34:4; Revelation 9:3; 9:5; 9:10; Deuteronomy 8:15

Libra (Scales)
Acts 9:18 Revelation 6:5 Leviticus 11:9-10, 11:12; 13:30-32; 13:35; 19:36; 22:22; Deuteronomy 14:9-10; 25:13; 1 Samuel 17:5; 1 Kings 22:34; ALSO Ezra 8:29; Job 6:2; Job 31:6; Job 41:15; Job 41:30; Psalm 26:2; 62:9 Proverbs 5:21; 11:1; 16:2; 16:11; 20:23; 21:22; Isaiah 40:12; 40:15; 46:6-7; Jeremiah 32:10; Ezekiel 5:1; 29:4; 45:10; Daniel 5:27; Hosea 12:7; Amos 8:5 Micah 6:11
Also: 510 mention of the word "justice" and 7,930 mention of the word "law"

Virgo/Virgin

Matthew 1:18; 1:23; 1:25; Luke 1:27; 1:34; 2:36 Acts 21:9 1 Corinthians 7:28; 7:34; 7:36-38; 2 Corinthians 11:2; Revelation 14:4; Genesis 19:8; 24:16; 24:43; 34:2; Exodus 2:8; 22:16; 22:17; 27:20; 29:40; Leviticus 21:3; 21:13-14; 24:2; Number 28:5; 31:35; 31:40; 31:46; Deuteronomy 22:14-15; 22:17; 22:19-20; 22:23-29; 32:25; Judges 11:37; 11:39; 19:24; 21:11; 2 Samuel 13:2; 13:18; 1 Kings 1:2; 2 Kings 19:21; 2 Chronicles 36:17; Esther 2:3; 2:12; Job 31:1; Psalm 45:14 Proverbs 30:19; Song of Solomon 8:9-10; Isaiah 7:14; 23:12; 37:22; 47:1; 62:5; Jeremiah 2:32; 14:17; 18:13; 31:4; 31:13; 31:21; 46:11; 51:22; Lamentations 1:15; 2:2; 2:13 Ezekiel 9:6; 23:3; 23:8; 44:22; Joel 1:8; Amos 5:

"I can only assume," NP said as he collected himself without missing a beat, that the 'land of 'milk and honey' refers to the bridge from the Milky Way Galaxy to the Beehive Cluster of stars in Cancer; after all, bees produce honey. Let's look at a few more sayings I've been jotting down here in the meantime. Mark 10:25: 'It's easier for a camel to go through the eye of a needle than for someone who is rich to enter the kingdom of God.' Well, this doesn't make much sense unless you're talking about the light of the star Camelopardalis passing through a needle. It would definitely be easier for that to happen than for a rich man to gain access to the kingdom of God; light would have no problem passing through that hole."

"You're reaching on that one," I said.

"Maybe. How about in Matthew when John the Baptist was described as wearing camel-hair clothing and having a leather belt? He ate wild honey? Camel is Camelopardalis; leather comes from the female Taurus a little lower on the wheel, and belt is Orion's Belt. Wild honey comes from the Beehive Cluster again. How about when Jesus walked on water? A person shouldn't have the ability to do that, but the Sun does it all the time." How about Proverbs 16:18: 'Pride comes before the fall'; well, a group of lions is called a pride, so if the Sun is in Leo, then it is actually right before the fall. Hold on…I want to show you one more thing." With that, he ran over to the papers on his desk and pulled this out:

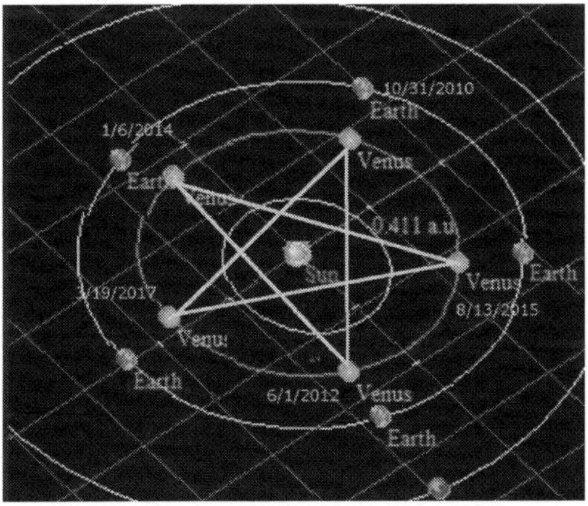

"Okay, this is the sun in the middle and Venus and Earth orbit around it. These five points are where the two planets are closest to each other in the orbits; it forms a pentagram," he said.

"So?" I inquired.

"Venus is called the morning star because it's the light you see rise to announce the arrival of God's Sun. Venus's other name is Lucifer. There's his pentagram."

My mind shot back to the letter. Peter: 1: 19-21: 'Continue until the day star rises in your hearts.' I began to understand the implications. Was this why my brother was killed? This is the heliopause of where faith ends and knowing begins. What else did he know? A rage started building up inside me. It was quickly put on pause by NP's spastic interruption. "There's some information I have at home that might be useful for the rest of the letter. I've been working on a section of it on my own time. I wasn't sure how it fit into this, but I see now. I'll be back," he said as he bolted out of the library.

Until that exact moment, it hadn't occurred to me that there was still half a letter to get through. As we started to gather ourselves to leave, Jean took a phone call. It didn't occur to me until this moment that there was a life outside of ours.

"Non, non je comprends, j'ai besoin de deux heures. Bon, je file maintenant. Hey, guys. I have to jet too. I just got a call from my dad. I totally forgot but I've got a business meeting he set up I have to attend. I'll bring food back to the room. My cell if you need me. I'll see you in a few hours."

While the girls and I tried to work out some more problems in this letter on the walk home, something became abundantly apparent. NP was light years smarter than us despite our collective intelligence. Getting to the bottom of this was going to be tricky while he was gone. Little did we know, that would be the last time any of us would see him alive.

CHAPTER 14

I plugged the watch in one last time to Rosette's Mizu. There was one file left. There was a password to access them. Question: Animal facing out right after ice age. He must have put a fail-safe in case someone caught this. Answer: Sphinx.

Day 3: My final thoughts; Part 1

Well done, Teddy. I knew you and "NP," as you lovingly call him, were too smart for your own good. This one is going to be the last one I write and consequently it's going to be a long one. I'm not sure how much longer I have here. I think they're onto the dips I take behind "enemy lines," though I'm not sure if they know I use the computer. By now you know the Bible is allegorically encoded. It goes without saying that free will is the choice of humanity. God gives us a choice, but what do all choices begin with? They begin with thought before it becomes intentions, words, actions, personality, etc. You know the saying, 'There is nothing new under the Sun?' I feel that sentence should have a bit more meaning for you now, but it's true. There is creation and discovery but everything is already there just waiting to be attained. Did planes not have the ability to fly well before they were created? Everything begins in thought—maybe that's the choice God gave us; maybe self-awareness is His greatest gift. It would surely explain why we're the only organism to carry those, no? I don't believe that non-conscious material evolves into consciousness being capable of self-awareness. But what you don't know yet is the tangential extent of allegory in the Bible. Let me show you two examples:

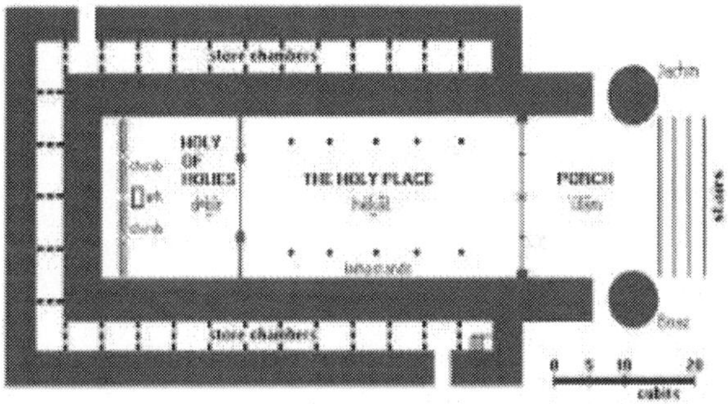

Here is the blueprint for King Solomon's temple; well, it should be if you follow the instructions in the Bible. Solomon was the king, but it's also a breakdown of three words: Sol, Ohm, and On. If you made it this far, bro, I know that you have evolved in your thinking, so stay with me. Sol is Latin for Sun, or light, where energy is found. It's why light was created on day one, the

*Sun*day, and why the day of rest in the Old Testament is the Saturday. Ohm that you hear Buddhists chant is the most sacred sound to be emitted. It represents the manifest and the un-manifested aspects of God. It's also 136.1 Hertz on a tuning fork that is used to stimulate the heart chakra, which also enables meditation through access of the pineal gland. On was the Egyptian name for the Greek city of the light, Heliopolis. If you put it all together, it is The Sun | of the City of Light | is within your heart | both manifesting and un-manifesting. Now what was said in Luke 17:21? "Neither shall they say, Lo here! Or, lo there! For, behold, the kingdom of God is within you." Now think about that. Incidentally, this is why now when you go into a dark room, you first have to turn the lights *on* before you can see anything.

Now I'm assuming by now you've become familiar with the solstices. But do you *really* know why they're on those specific days? Or how it ties into this all? There are two solstices. June 21st is the longest day of the year, as it's the beginning of summer. However, I'm more interested in discussing the other solstice. On December 21st, winter starts and is the shortest day of the year. Winter also symbolically begins the 'death of God's sun.' Stay close. On December 22nd, the sun rises on the lowest degree of the year. It rises on the same identical degree on the 23rd, as well as the 24th. That's three days in a row that the sun will rise on the identical degree. This is why it's been documented that they used to say that 'God's sun was dead for three days' and on the fourth day, which is December 25th—his birthday, incidentally—it rises an additional degree and will continue to rise a degree a day on the horizon until June 21, when it will then stop for three days again and start to decline on the 25th. In Job, he asks: 'Do you know when the wild goats give birth?' Well December 25th, the birth of Christ, in Capricorn, the goat. This is also why anything that could come back to life after being dead was "born again," and was always born on December 25th.

This brings me to my climax. There are people in this world who control the truth to these books and this information and who benefit from it not getting out; I'm talking about the following:

"ALL FORMS OF DIVINATION ARE TO BE REJECTED: RECOURSE TO SATAN OR DEMONS, CONJURING UP THE DEAD, OR OTHER PRACTICES FALSELY SUPPOSED TO 'UNVEIL' THE FUTURE. **CONSULTING HOROSCOPES**, **ASTROLOGY**, PALM READING, INTERPRETATION OF OMENS AND LOTS, THE PHENOMENA OF CLAIRVOYANCE, AND RECOURSE TO MEDIUMS ALL CONCEAL A DESIRE FOR POWER OVER TIME, HISTORY, AND, IN THE LAST ANALYSIS, OTHER HUMAN

BEINGS, AS WELL AS A WISH TO CONCILIATE HIDDEN POWERS. THEY CONTRADICT THE HONOR, RESPECT, AND LOVING FEAR THAT WE OWE TO GOD ALONE" (CATECHISM OF THE ROMAN CATHOLIC CHURCH 2116)

You lived in DC for a few years. Before the Supreme Court commences, they have a service called Red Mass. This takes place every year before SCOTUS is in session and is where they pray to Saint Thomas More for guidance over law and justice. Thomas More was the one who burned William Tyndale at the stake. Well, William Tyndale was the sole person charged by King James to translate the Bible from Latin to English; in fact, the King James Bible is mostly entirely his verbiage. The Catholic (which is Latin for Universal, incidentally) Church used to have it chained to the pews and would burn people to death who would try and read or translate it. They had a monopoly on it since the very beginning of Christianity. Nonetheless, the King wanted the Bible translated so he commissioned Tyndale to translate it. Orders from the Pope had him killed by More, upon which King James had More killed for failing to follow the King's orders. Tyndale's final words were, "Lord, open their eyes" Two things happened around this time; one piggybacked off the other. One was the Gutenberg press; the second, with the Bible now accessible to the masses, was the Protestant Reformation. Fast forward to now. Once a year, a special mass is held to pray to a saint who torched the person who was trying to bring the Bible to mass consciousness. The Red Mass that opens SCOTUS prays to More, who is the "Heavenly Patron of Statesmen and Politicians."

I have to run now, Teddy. I could honestly go on forever, but they're probably sending a search out for me again. At least now you know how to look for symbolism. They have to be onto me by now. I love you, Teddy. I hope I've shed some light on this. I'm so proud of you. I know you were used to seeing me as this womanizing animal, but the truth is that I would have given anything to find something as treasured as what you have with Hannah. Don't let her go.

Peace and Love,

—J

It was as I finished reading it that my cell phone rang with a call I never thought I'd receive in my life for the second time in a week. The phone snapped me out of my daze.

"Yes, this is him. EXCUSE ME? No, no. I'll be right over. We have to go. There's been an accident at NP's," I screeched.

"WHAT? What happened?"

"They…um. His roommate. FUCK. Sorry! His neighbor found him on the floor in the living room not breathing; the door was open; a bottle of pills in his hand and…um… we have to go.”

CHAPTER 15

"Do you think we made the right call, Roger? I feel terrible that we didn't tell Jake about the meeting," Lilac said nervously.

"Absolutely, Madam President. Plausible deniability. He'll have that on his side. It's not like it's the first thing you've kept from him; why are you having such difficulty with this one?"

"Because I thought we had this all wrapped up nice and tight the first time," Lilac said as she fumbled around for her e-cigarette. Oh fuck this, she thought, as she pulled out a fresh piece of Nicorette. Anything but cigarettes. She was intent on keeping her promise even as the stresses of her daily job were getting the better of her.

"Lilly, you look awful. What happened? I've just been going over your speech tomorrow and couldn't find you anywhere. Is everything all right?" Jake asked.

"No, I'm fine, Jake. Thank you for asking. I just got sidetracked with a few things. It's so hard to get some air in here. Over a hundred rooms and it feels smaller than my first dorm at

Columbia. How is that even possible?"

"Because all you had to deal with was homework and freshman hipsters. Things are a little bigger on this side of the Rose Garden, aren't they?"

"You're not helping, Jake," she said as she chewed furiously on her piece of gum.

"Madam President, you're going to want to hear this," Roger interrupted. "It's about James Newsdon."

"Tell me."

"It's better if we go in the conference room," Roger replied.

As they walked down the corridor to the conference room, Lilac felt herself allowing herself to re-grow that knot in her stomach that was there before. Why wouldn't this kid go away? It was almost an impossible burden on her to have to deal with this and worry about her speech to Congress tomorrow. I guess this was important enough that they bothered her with her hair let down.

"This better be good," she said.

"Oh, it is," Roger replied. "Our contacts overseas put out pictures of James all around and it turned out a local kid recognized him. He had asked him for a ride over the border to the Netherlands. He paid him a thousand American dollars to take him to Amsterdam, no questions asked."

"This is perfect. Because nothing wild ever

happens in Amsterdam," Lilac said. She had a feeling that the kid didn't go there for the pot and mushrooms. "Well, did he take a flight out of Amsterdam using one of his passports?" she asked.

"We have no indication that he ever left Amsterdam. He was there for maybe two days tops and then caught a ride back with some kids to Cologne. This just came in from the train station in Cologne," Roger said as he put up a closed-circuit camera shot of James wearing a hoodie and a three-day shave, looking directly at the counter person. "From Cologne, he made his way to Berlin, where he then took a flight back to his location. One of his boys must have picked him up at the airport," Roger finished.

"What the hell is in Amsterdam besides sex, drugs, and the Anne Frank museum?" Lilac mused out loud.

"We're not sure yet. We've started asking around, but finding out what he did there might prove difficult. He paid with cash and we have no idea where he stayed. We don't even know if he stayed there the whole time," Roger puffed.

"Well, this is perfect. Please let me know when you actually have something to report," Lilac said as she turned to leave.

"This might be good news, actually," Jake said optimistically.

"How is any of this good, Jake?"

"He only spent two days in Amsterdam. He

lost time on the drive there; he had only cash. Maybe he just went there to unwind. You know how these kids are," Jake replied.

Truth was she knew exactly how they are and they don't just try and disappear off the grid for a few days without something to do. But he hadn't used his military e-mail and nothing had come in and out of his brother's e-mail in the last three months, well before all this started. Graham was in school at the time and there was no way that any of those kids were in Holland, Amsterdam, or anywhere near Germany. What in the holy hell was going on there? More importantly, what secret could this kid possibly possess that would be so important that he would risk his life and welfare for?

CHAPTER 16

We pulled up to NP's block. I hadn't been there in weeks. It looked a little more destitute since I had last been there. There was a man ringing a Salvation Army bell outside the restaurant next to his building. Rose must have seen the anger in my face.

"Wow. Okay, sweetie, you're going to have to pull yourself together or you're going to get pinkie-cuffed to the furnace."

I took a few deep breaths and tried to calm down, but this was just not going to happen. This was my best friend we were talking here. As soon as I walked in, I started getting accosted by this giant round fellow, Officer Hitchlords. He took a liking to me right away.

"You're Newsdon, right?" he said.

"How's NP doing?" I said, ignoring his question.

"Pierce? He was gone before we got here. In the corner. I'm sorry."

Everything in my life froze; I couldn't breathe. I just kept playing back the last thing I said to him. "Thanks for all your help, man," was hardly the last thing I wanted to say. How about thanks for always being there for me; thanks for never giving up on me; thanks for putting up with me when I was hammered all those times; thanks for having a sense of humor; thanks for...

"Are you in there?" Hitchlords slapped me out of my trance.

"What?" I said.

"We are going to need you to come downtown and answer some questions," he replied.

"Excuse me?" I said.

"The pills he has in his hand are aspirin. This would be fantastic if he was looking to donate his heart, but you see the foam around his mouth and his super red skin. The M.E. says that's in line with cyanide poisoning."

The cop stopped talking. Clearly he wanted me to lead this conversation a bit. Was this fat, stereotypical cop trying to tell me that my friend was murdered? I decided to play dumb for him.

"Are you saying that he killed himself with cyanide then held a bottle of pills to throw you off track?" God it feels so good to play dumb sometimes.

"You've got to be the dumbest Harvard kid of all time. We'll do the rest of this downtown," he said and motioned me to the door.

"Why does every typical cop conversation have to go like that? "Listen, unless I am under arrest, I am not going anywhere with you. Not now, not never, and I was with other people for the last…forever. So there's your alibi, as well as my refusal to do anything further," I said. Then I threw in the kicker to really edge him off: "Does he have any Sambuca left in the freezer?" Boy, that turned his douche meter all the way up.

"This is a crime scene, asshole; you touch anything, you *will* go downtown. You want to explain to me why he had a cell phone in his hand with your number up on the screen?"

Wait what? Unreal, but there it was, my number on his phone.

"Care to explain that?" he remarked snidely.

"Because we're best friends. Do you care to explain why this looks exactly like a *DaVinci Code* murder scene and you are blaming me for a suicide? In fact, he left me a little while ago and was planning to come back. I was actually expecting him before you called. Jean!" I screamed, perhaps a bit too loud.

"Merde, merde que c'est-il passe ici?" he said.

"Pierce killed himself." Rosette said, fighting back tears.

"Quoi?"

"Or he was killed and it was staged like a suicide; we have no idea." I replied. I had a sudden urge for a cigarette, though I don't smoke. "Where have you been?" I asked.

"Job interview. I told you. I'm interning at Saturnalian Watermark at the Square for the rest of the year," he boasted proudly. Not like we didn't see this coming a mile away, with his connections. Of course he was. He probably wouldn't even finish business school. He'll come out of that internship starting at three-fifty a year. "They just called me out of nowhere," he finished

"Don't be modest, Solex," Rosette said.

"All right, fine. Can we stop talking about me? What do we know so far?" he asked.

"Can I break this love fest up? the fat cop interrupted.

"I clearly didn't do this. Can I go now?" I was becoming irritated at the lack of personality on the guy.

"I recognize you from TV. Your brother was the one killed overseas in that ambush, right? I'm sorry for your loss. I have the utmost respect for soldiers. But you want to explain to me why a week later you are standing in your best friend's apartment, your phone information up on his cell and mentioned in the suicide letter?"

I followed white Carl Winslow over to it; well, dragged myself over was more like it. My feet felt like Stonehenge boulders. I felt like I was sleeping, like this wasn't happening. Maybe this was that floating-away disassociation feeling NP talked about when you experience a trauma you can't handle. After what seemed like eternity, I stopped right in front of the table and looked down at this piece of paper:

Graham,
The key to peace is in my music. Tell Rosette that I will always love her and I know how she really felt about me. I'm sorry but I couldn't take it anymore. I bequeath to you the new *Dracula* DVD and my Monte Cristo in the fridge. I'm sorry but I had no choice. Seek out the jester.
—NP

Let me just ask. Put yourselves in my shoes. After all that had happened to my brain that week, how would you have reacted? What would you have thought? What would your next mental process be?

"I need a drink right now," I blurted out.

"That's what we've heard," Officer Hitchlords retorted.

"Excuse me?" I replied angrily.

"We showed your picture to the local bars, trying to piece this together, and every tender not only knew you by name, but what credit card you have. Do I need to tell you not to go far or leave the country in case we have any questions?" he finished.

"Whatever you say. can I use the bathroom before we go, or am I going to have to do it in the alleyway outside by the Salvation Army guy and have you arrest me?" I snarled. I suddenly had a flashback to that public urination ticket I got a few years back. Where was all this hate for stock-character cop coming from?

"They're finished in there. You've got thirty seconds. Kids these days have no respect for authority. The shield means nothing anymore." He sighed.

I shuffled into the bathroom and did my business. I felt dizzy so I sat down on the toilet for a minute. I looked to my left and noticed NP's Nautical 2.0 music player. I fumbled with it for a minute. It was one of those that didn't tell you what songs were coming up. I needed something to take my mind off this. The key to peace is in his music. It better be, I thought. I rolled the buds into my ears and walked out of the bathroom, then kept walking past everyone into the backseat of the car.

The drive home was uneventful. Hannah went with Jean and I stayed with Rose. I guess they figured they didn't want us fighting because of this, but I'm just guessing. The entire time Rose just listened to her Rising CD. I had on NP's Nautical. What in the hell kind of Bohemian crap was this? I took a swig out of the Orange Grove juice I took from the fridge when Hitch turned around. Fuck him. It definitely didn't calm me down on the ride home. I walked into the house and went directly for the bottle of SoCo I kept hidden in the cookie jar. Poured myself the entire thing on ice. Walked into the middle of the room, Nautical still blasting Bohemian bullshit. I looked at the glass, then I remembered what NP said about me boozing and I felt this ball of anger build from the pit of my solar plexus and manifest at the speed of light to my Adam's apple, where I felt a heartbeat explode. I turned to the kitchen wall with the glass and launched it at hard as I could, alcohol flying, glass shattering. I fell on my knees and started to cry for the first time since my parents separated and it just wouldn't stop. Hannah, probably thinking a wild animal broke in and was masturbating in the living room, flew up the stairs to find me in that pathetic state on the floor. She cleaned up the mess I had just made and spent the next hour soothing and calming me down. I lay on the couch with her cradling me until I passed out.

"We're going to get through this together, baby. I know it's a lot. I'm here for you. I'll always be here for you. We'll figure this out," she soothed as my world turned black.

Act justly, love mercy, walk humbly
—Micah 6:8

CHAPTER 17
(ONE MONTH LATER)

I had somehow managed to channel all my energy back into my classes and had aced my exams. By day, I put all my energy into medicine. By night, I was into everything NP was into. Blur was on TV 24/7; I was trolling all the alternative sites. I still couldn't figure out what he meant by his music, though. I figured in due time. I also had become a bit of a shut-in. SeaMart has this grocery delivery service called "the current." I didn't even have to leave the room. Unfortunately, I forgot that Rose had a key to the apartment and four to five weeks is roughly the longest period of time I've gone without seeing her. I'm lucky I still had my teeth in my face. She decided to make her presence felt this particular Friday night.

"Hey asshole, you don't answer your phone or come out to…oh my God. What happened to your hair?" she said, shocked.

Right, so I hadn't shaved in about a month or so.

"I switched shampoos," I said.

"What?" she replied.

"I was using Head & Shoulders and my hair was going from my head to my shoulders. Now the problem's solved," I said.

"Is that right, Nostradumbass?"

"Let me tell you a little story about the Native Americans and why they grew their hair long. A study was done during the Vietnam War in which they sent people to reservations looking for Native Americans to join the war on our side," I said.

"Are you on something right now?" She took a step back, concerned.

"Their awesome skills in hunting and survival disappeared once they cut their long hair. Just vanished. However, those with the long hair were able to feel an enemy with another sense they couldn't explain. Only it disappeared when they got their buzz cuts," I finished proudly. Not sure why; I didn't exactly make a strong point.

"I think you need to Occupy barbershop…maybe Occupy chainsaw. Get up and get dressed."

"They mention it in the Bible. Story of Samson. Once his hair is cut, his powers are gone. The above is military, documented phenomenon," I continued.

"Whatever excites you. What exactly have you been up to? This place looks like a frat bomb went off," she asked.

"Learning. Have you heard this theory of the reptilians?"

"Yeah, I wrote a paper on it not too long ago: about how these people can mistake MacLean's Triune Reptilian Midbrain for lizards wearing people skin. Occupy Petco? goddamn it, Graham!" She waddled through the books and blankets on the floor, right up to me, and slapped me in the face and pushed me onto the couch. Not that she probably couldn't give me a run for my money, as fit and strong as she was, but I was not expecting it and I almost broke my neck on the back of the couch.

"What the hell was that all about? What's wrong with you?" I snapped.

"Did your long hair sense that coming, beardo? No? I've got a better question. What's wrong with you? Your best friend dies a month ago and you just go off the map. Everything you've worked toward just thrown out the window so you can chase non-linear information like some hippie dabbling at a library? It's great that you're studying about dinomen; I'm sure it makes for great role play with Husker. You know, maybe you're a T. rex who's angry because your arms are too short and you can't take your pants off and you need Miss Brontosoreass to come help; but, if you haven't noticed, or maybe were once again too hammered to notice, your best friend left you a coded letter."

"I haven't had a drink since he died," I replied coldly.

"Do you really think if Pierce knew he was going to be killed and was forced to write a suicide note, as smart as he was, he would not have identified who it was in it? Do you ever learn anything? Did that note sound normal to you? I know you had tests and classes to get through, but now that finals are over, you have no excuse." With that, she cleaned up the area, went behind the TV, and brought out the two boards. One was completely filled with my brother's note. On the other, she wrote out the entire suicide note.

"Right off the bat, do you see anything odd with this note?" she asked.

"Um…"

"Come on, Graham. WAKE UP!"

"Yes, okay? Yes. Of course. Why would he give me a movie and a sandwich? Also, I can't figure out his music at all; I've been listening to his mp3 player for a month now."

"Now you're on track, I'm so glad I don't have to throw this at you and mess up your pretty little face." Holiday roast coffee with almond milk. Girl knows me inside out. "Here is the part that really got me that you missed. I took a look at the suicide letter when you went into the bathroom and the front of the letter said, 'Caught in the Gorgon Stare.' It just seemed, I dunno, profound and out of place. So I looked it up. It's a DARPA Mind's Eye project. Mind's eye. Like the pineal gland. Anyway. It's a drone that has sixty-five eyeballs on it. Can take an entire city in pictures," she said.

"A little unnecessary, no?" I asked.

"It gets better. Gorgon in Greek mythology was a three-headed monster. Stheno and Euryale were immortal; their sister was not. Do you know who she was?" she asked. I was getting sick of mythology by now. "Have you heard of Medusa?"

"Get out of here. You're telling me there is a drone named after Medusa?" I replied.

"The idea is when you look up and see it, you 'turn to stone,' aka lose your life. Isn't that sick?" She said.

"That's probably the most twisted thing I've heard so far." I was being serious.

"Then that got me thinking and reminded me of something I'd almost forgotten. Who else used to use a ton of cameras and tell us never to look directly into them? "Don't stare directly into the camera, boy." She put on her best deep voice.

"The only one I can think of, I guess, would be Rosibuild for the debates," I said.

"Bingo! He would record everything and if someone had a good idea during a debate, he would write about it and get published. He would keep the tapes and film his class lectures around this person's good idea and line the tapes up so that it looked it was his idea in case the student tried to call him out. Who would believe a kid? Remember when Pierce was in tenth grade and was in his twelfth-grade class and he came home that day pissed off because Rosibuild stole an idea from him? I still remember his idea. He said that Washington, being a Freemason and technically the first president, was put on the dollar note and on the quarter. Hamilton was the first treasury secretary and established the national bank. The central bankers didn't like that so he was killed by a former vice president and the moneymakers and was thereby honored by being put on the ten-dollar bill. Andrew Jackson's famous last words were: 'I killed the bank,' meaning his fighting off the second national bank and since the Federal Reserve private bank was enacted, the elites memorialized him on the twenty-dollar bill just to spite him. Lincoln was about to print greenbacks instead of using the central bank, was killed, and then was commemorated by being put on the penny and on the five-dollar bill. Woodrow Wilson, the one who enacted the Federal Reserve Act of 1913 and gave the US over to private bankers, was rewarded by becoming the face of the hundred-thousand-dollar bill. Lastly, Kennedy, who signed executive order 11110 to print silver-backed money and get us off the Federal Reserve, was killed and now is on the fifty-cent coin.

Rosibuild took that and turned it into the Boston conspiracy story of the year, remember? That stupid award he kept on his desk that looked like a giant glass dick with a lazy eye in the middle of it?" I was impressed with her memory.

"How do you remember all of this?" I asked.

"For one, I actually was sober throughout high school. Also, he was the only guy who ever treated me worth a shit. He loved me and I knew this. I just couldn't let myself realize it back. I was stupid. Also, we were partners in that class; he's two years younger than us—was two years younger than us. Anyway, I went home after the last time I saw you and dug into my high school paperwork. "If the American people ever allow private banks to control the issue of their currency, first by inflation, then by deflation, the banks and corporations that will grow up around them will deprive the people of all property until their children wake up homeless on the continent their fathers conquered...I believe that banking institutions are more dangerous to our liberties than standing armies... The issuing power should be taken from the banks and restored to the people, to whom it properly belongs." That was Thomas Jefferson, face of the defunct two-dollar bill and the nickel. Do you think there's a bit more to who gets put on money than is being left off?" she asked angrily, still just as hurt as the day she lost him.

"I'm so sorry, Rose" was all I could say.

"It's too late for that now. Pierce got caught in the stare. The good news is unlike the other two: Medusa isn't immortal and I think I know how we can cut her head off."

"You know, honestly, I really have to know this because it's driving me crazy. Let me just plug this Nautical in and take the band names and songs down. Maybe we can go through them together and see what he's talking about because listening to this over and over again is going to give me a seizure," I said. I plugged the Nautical into the Mizu because I hadn't charged my Shui in the past month. I had to wait a minute and let it connect with her program. The icon for the Nautical popped up. Then this crazy idea popped into my head. I had a flashback to the first time I discovered the flash-drive watch. I clicked on the music player and opened it as a drive. I sank back in my chair and heard Rosette squeal. At least I'd never have to listen to this awful music again. There were a bunch of files titled "Rose" and numbered. Two were titled "Doc." I opened the smaller one first. The answer was in his music after all.

Doc 1: What's Up, Doc?

If this is something you are reading, something has happened to me. Call it crazy paranoia like you always did, but you're reading this now, aren't you? You don't just get to know how the world works behind the scenes without either pulling the strings or being on a shit list. I'm not sure how a peaceful society would work because there has been war since the dawn of modern civilization. Billy Joel was right. Only the good die young. Well, not really. They're rubbed off this planet. Then we enshrine them. Seems a bit hypocritical, no? What did Bob Marley say? How long shall they kill our prophets while we stand aside and look? Why do people like Blur Slanders, which incidentally is just an anagram for Bulls Errands, aka working for the papal bulls in Rome, go on TV with their supreme vocabulary preaching fighting the revolution and be allowed to continue without any consequences. It's because agitation and state of war is the name of the game. People are taught hate and closed mindedness instead of how to think about things that are interesting and that nobody considers.

I hope you don't mind, but I have been working on decoding a section of this letter myself. Once I saw my name in it, I knew it was for me to figure out. Your brother had a special mind, let me tell you.

Viva la peaceful disobedience,
Nerds (NP)
P.S.: Tell Rose I'm sorry I've been too much of a bitch to send these to her but to forgive me anyway.

"These" must be love letters. They are going to have to wait. Sorry, Rose.

Doc 2:

Reminds me of that kid from *Family Ties*. You don't have to have "FAMILY TIES" to be one of the family. November 5. Just
remember…remember. Words aren't chosen by accident. You may want to sit down for this one. No? Okay. Your choice. Remember, remember, the 5th of November is a quote symbolizing the famous attempt to blow up Parliament. The gunpowder plot? He was mentioning my family ties, my name. My last name is Pierce, but it was changed over from Percy when the English settlers came over. The Percy family was directly involved in the gunpowder plot. My mother always told me I had some wealthy family members who we didn't talk to.

You've heard of the Anonymous movement, right? The masks, the auto-tune voices? Hackers. Their work helps uncover pedophile rings and hack into government sites; it's a bunch of non-sequitur work really. But it's not centralized so it should be expected as such. Just a bunch of unrelated works with no end game and no centralized agreement of plans. Remember the scene in *A Princess Bride* where Inigo Montoya says, "I have been in the revenge business for twenty years. Now that it's over, I don't know what to do?" Methinks it's the same shit. Check this out.

The rule of the church and the movements we see today can be summed up entirely by the *Count of Monte Cristo.*

In fact, it's interesting that most Anonymous people do not question the following that has been built into their mindset:

1) Fawkes was a Catholic who was involved in a failed assassination attempt on King James. That's right. Here is a Catholic who tried to kill the King who was responsible for good or, worse, having the Bible commissioned and translated into English. Had he not done this, the Bible could very well still be in Latin, chained to the pew, and interpretations handed out in church. This is right at the cusp of the Protestant Reformation and the printing press, which came about eighty-five years before. That's the equivalent of us talking about policies enacted in 1932 and how still it affects us. To put it into perspective: we still talk openly about our grandparents, the Great Depression, Babe Ruth, and Hitler, don't we?

All right. Maybe not in the same sentence; at least I hope not. Fawkes was led by a Jesuit named Robert Catesby. The question is, why is this movement of exposing the government being back-masked (pun intended) on a Jesuit mission, knowing that they are behind everything nowadays? (Don't worry, I will get to that.)

2) This was a total failed mission. Why is he the face of a new mission to undermine a government corruption if his mission failed miserably? He was in charge of watching the gunpowder, got caught on an anonymous (pun intended again...I'm getting good at this) tip. He then spilled the beans. Only then did he jump to his death instead of waiting to be hung. He wasn't a hero.
3) The mask, it is produced by a large US TV conglomerate that makes profit every time one gets bought.
4) Nobody finds it ironic that in *V for Vendetta,* the one movie they watch, is the *Count of Monte Cristo* multiple times?" Let me educate you a bit more.

Alexander Dumas, who wrote *The Count of Monte Cristo* fought in 1848 to free Rome from the power of the Pope and wrote a ton of books to expose this. The Count was a Jesuit general. Monte=mount, Cristo=Christ. Good so far? Alexander was referring to the general getting revenge when the Jesuits were suppressed. In real life, Pope Clement XII expelled the Jesuits and shipped them off when he got tired of their shit. It was only when Pope Pius VII reinstated them in 1814 that they were allowed back. Back to the story: many of them were sent to an island off Portugal. When they finally were reinstated, they got rid of all the European powers that had pushed them out in the first place. So when you read this book, keep in mind that it's really just a convoluted satire on the Jesuits getting their power back and not just some Don Juan sexy-time book. It's another allegory, like the Bible has been shown to be. At the end of the book, the Count doesn't get what he wants, what we all crave, which is the love of another. He doesn't get the girl. He gets his power and everything he lost, but he does not get his lady. To have a woman and a family makes you vulnerable. It means anyone can use them against you. Family always outweighs the choices of the general and that is why they will never be married, which is why they are so powerful. Now we're in a time where the first Jesuit pope was ever elected. He's also the first pope from outside of Europe in over 1300 years. Have you ever wondered why a pope has never been nominated for a Nobel Peace Prize? They tried to push for it vigorously a while back and the committee ended up spurning them and giving it to a woman instead, to add insult to injury. Plus, you're talking the Supreme Court. Two-thirds of them are Roman Catholic and at least half of them were educated or hold adjunct professorships at Jesuit schools.

I made you watch *V for Vendetta*, right? Is there now any doubt why they watch the *Count of Monte Cristo* multiple times in the movie? Now think to the end. V could have stayed with Evey and sent the train with the explosives to cripple them all and blow up Parliament, but instead he went in as 'the idea; the movement" and ended up losing his life. The movement won, but he never got the woman. Now why would the Anonymous movement attach themselves to a Jesuit figurehead order that tried to kill the King who wanted to bring the Bible to mass consciousness? The movement might be skewed, although well intentioned, but ask yourself if the mask was selected on purpose. James said he was confused at first and kept blamin' these feelings on the "brews"? Alcohol? Nope. The Hebrews. No, he followed his instinct and his instinct told him all about her. Jess, you it? Almost. How about Jesuit. Keeps this writing on him at all times or, as he puts it, "until I mail." Close. It's an anagram for Illuminati. He used shorthand, compound sounds, and anagrams to get his message across.

Also, last but not least, it's important to know that the powers that be in this world have inserted Ophiuchus as the thirteenth sign to bury all this information. Know that the perfect cross, or the cross of God's Sun that forms when you intersect the solstices with the equinoxes, does not form a perfect cross when you have included Ophiuchus.

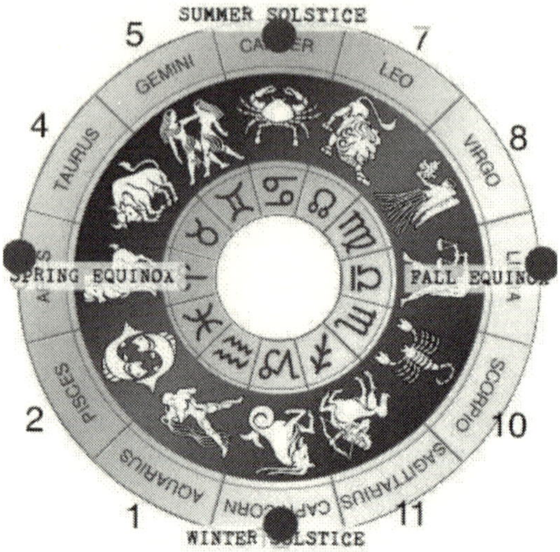

If you look back in history, the zodiac never included Ophiuchus and in this way the code was always there, ready to be decoded. Now suddenly they've decided that the zodiac has been wrong all this time? I could go into all the ways this addition masks the information in the Bible, but I just don't have that time. Just believe me that it only serves to make it harder to get the right information out there.

—Your best friend, NP

Rosette and I just stood there staring at each other. Ninety-five percent of the letter was done and this warm, overpowering feeling came over me. I looked into her eyes.

"We have to go head back to Rosibuild's," I said.

"It's the middle of the day; he's at Interlock right now. Why?" she asked.

"He said to seek out the Jester. Also, I didn't say he was going to be home. We are going to tear this guy's house apart. If words aren't an accident, and he was there when NP died, we're going to find proof."

"The Jesuits are a MILITARY organization, not a religious order. Their chief is a general of an army, not the mere father abbot of a monastery. And the aim of this organization is power—power in its most despotic exercise—absolute power, universal power, power to control the world by the volition of a single man [i.e., the Black Pope, the Superior General of the Jesuits]. Jesuitism is the most absolute of despotisms [sic]—and at the same time the greatest and most enormous of abuses..."

—Napoleon Bonaparte

"The Jesuits...are simply the Romish army for the earthly sovereignty of the world in the future, with the Pontiff of Rome for emperor...that's their ideal.... It is simple lust of power, of filthy earthly gain, of domination—something like a universal serfdom with them [i.e., the Jesuits] as masters—that's all they stand for. They don't even believe in God perhaps."

—Fyodor Dostoyevsky

"My history of the Jesuits is not eloquently written, but it is supported by unquestionable authorities, [and] is very particular and very horrible. Their [the Jesuit Order's] restoration [in 1814 by Pope Pius VII] is indeed a step toward darkness, cruelty, despotism, [and] death.... I do not like the appearance of the Jesuits. If ever there was a body of men who merited eternal damnation on earth and in hell, it is this Society of [Ignatius de] Loyola."

—John Adams [in a letter to Thomas Jefferson]

"The war [i.e., the American Civil War of 1861-1865] would never have been possible without the sinister influence of the Jesuits. We owe it to popery that we now see our land reddened with the blood of her noblest sons. Though there were great differences of opinion between the South and the North on the question of slavery, neither Jeff Davis [President of the Confederacy] nor anyone of the leading men of the Confederacy would have dared to attack the North, had they not relied on the promises of the Jesuits, that under the mask of Democracy, the money and arms of the Roman Catholic, even the arms of France, were at their disposal if they would attack us. I pity the priests, the bishops and monks of Rome in the United States, when the people realize that they are, in great part, responsible for the tears and the bloodshed in this war. I conceal what I know on that subject from the knowledge of the nation, for if the people knew the whole truth, this war would turn into a religious war, and it would at once take a tenfold more savage and bloody character."

—Abraham Lincoln (sixteenth president)

"They [i.e., the Jesuits] are educated men, prepared, and sworn to start at any moment, and in any direction, and for any service, commanded by the general of their order [i.e., the Jesuit Superior General, the "Black Pope"], bound to no family, community, or country, by the ordinary ties which bind men; and sold for life to the cause of the Roman Pontiff."

—Samuel Morse (inventor of the telegraph)

"Above all I have learned from the Jesuits. And so did Lenin too, as far as I recall. The world has never known anything quite so splendid as the hierarchical structure of the [Roman] Catholic Church. There were quite a few things I simply appropriated from the Jesuits for the use of the [Nazi] Party. The Catholic Church must be held up as an example. ...I will tell you a secret. I am founding an order In [Heinrich] Himmler. I see our Ignatius de Loyola."

—Adolf Hitler

CHAPTER 18

Oh, good. Perfect timing; there goes the doorknob.

"Behold, a dark horse!" I shouted.

"Damn, boy, you scared me half to death! What the hell are you doing in my house?" Rosibuild mustered.

"What's that they call you exactly? Your title since you officially left the order? the Beekeeper?" I said.

"Are you feeling all right, boy? Here, let me fix you a drink. Vanilla vodka and Red Bull. That's what you used to drink in my class all the time, right? I never turned you in; you were so damn intelligent during the debates, I couldn't get rid of a smart mind like yours, despite your demons." He tried turning the tide on me. Good thing I brought a master of psychology with me.

"I don't think so; we're here to talk about what you've done." I said.

"I've had enough of this right now. I have no idea what you're talking about. But you'd better get out of here. I've got things to do. I'm giving you one chance to leave on your own, or you're going out in handcuffs." He picked up the phone to dial.

"Before you do that, I have a theory, Mr. Rosibuild. Would you like to hear it? The truth is never told during the nine-to-five hours. Let's play a little game. Well, it's not really a game, but I'll give you the rules anyway. Let's pretend that while you were at work today, I didn't break into your house, go into your attic, find your secret stash of tapes, watch them, digitize them, then upload them to a private server. I was especially impressed by the one where you filmed my friend and ordered him off camera to write a suicide note and take a cyanide pill while my friend of six years, Jean, was in our graduation robe and hat and pointing a gun at him. Can't tell you how fantastic that made me feel," I asked calmly.

"That's crazy talk," he replied.

"You're right. I just made all that up. Something came over me and all that came out of absolutely nowhere. Temporarily possessed. Do you still do exorcisms? Don't worry; I'm not going to the police. See if I turn this over to the cops or the proper authorities, they'll know I have it, I've seen it, and who knows what they'll do to it, or even to me. But if I go ahead and scramble our location and signal, then all I have to do is send out a few e-mails from this dummy account I made with your information I found lying around the house and it'll be all over the Web, just like those banana-hammock pictures from Cabo we found. Although, as fat as you are, that might not be a banana hammock and you might have just tripped trying to get out of a hammock. I can't really tell. Killed my appetite. Incidentally, we partook in some of your delicious crackers and trilateral dip while watching your movies; hope you don't mind. Rose, if he moves, you know what to do. Incidentally, I did mention that this is a bucket of water and this…well, this right here is a Taser gun. You do understand how water and electricity work together, don't you? You know what, you do! Yes, that's right. I've seen the tapes. Oh, wait. That's crazy talk, right? Can we cut the shit and get down to it? I'm losing my patience with you!"

"Wait, wait, wait. All right, you've made your point. Where do you want to go from here? What do you want?" he pleaded.

"What I want, you can't give back. My cozy life. I can't unlearn the things I know now; the damage has been done. My best friend and brother are gone. Plus, I trusted you. Since you can't fix this, I've just made you my bitch for all eternity. Just so you know, I've sent the entire torrent file to the four corners of the Earth with a timer. If I don't reset it once a month, it gets released. It'll be everywhere and it will be back traced right back to you. So, don't think about sending someone after me. How you think this will play out?" I continued, driving my point in while Rosette clicked the Taser a few times.

"You ain't got no proof it was actually me. Could have been anybody," he finally said.

"I did mention that I walked around your house with the camera first, filming the entire house, taking in all the sights, pictures, family, extended family. In plain sight, right, Rosibuild? I mean, that's what you always told us. Then I pulled down the attic steps, went upstairs, and saw your little setup. The attic? Really? All those tapes. What would your dead wife think?" I was pissed he was still trying to weasel his way out of it.

"You mother…" he started

"Save your crap." With that, I calmly unscrewed the back of his laptop I was using and removed the hard drive. "Now, I'm going to keep this. I hope you don't mind. Love to see what else you have on it, plus, like I said, I don't need you getting any fresh ideas. Here's how it's going to work. You're going to retire immediately. Also, you're going to find that giant glass award that you stole from NP Forgive me, I didn't have time to trash this place for it. Next, you're going to donate half of your 401 or whatever's left of it to the Zip Code Bandits," I said.

"If I do that, you will leave me alone. You won't turn me in?" he said. Finally we were in the home stretch.

"If you do that, you have my word that I will not turn you in," I said.

"All right," he replied.

He did the walk-of-shame shuffle back up to

the attic and returned with the award a few minutes later.

"Newsdon," he shouted as we were leaving.

"What?" I turned around.

"I really did like you, boy. You do understand that this was not my call. They took my wife from me. I don't get to make the rules," he said.

"That's something that you'll have to live with," I said as we calmly left.

"Do you think he knows that you've installed streaming cameras in his overhead fire alarms?" Rosette asked.

"I believe this award should go to you. Oh, regarding that. Yeah, I think I'll watch him sweat it out a bit. Also, don't forget about the coat-hook cameras. I said that I'm not turning him in and I'm a man of my word. But I never said you shouldn't avenge NP. You don't just participate in taking a human life on this Earth then get blackmailed into doing something good and expect to live your life out. He's learned nothing; he's just scared of consequences. Bastards like him don't deserve leniency," I said, my confidence growing.

We went home and plugged the hard drive into my reader, then into her tablet. There were so many files of rules for rituals, financial records, and hidden bullion receipts, favors owed to and owed by nations. That could wait. I found the folder was titled "Newsdon." I clicked on it and there was one document titled

"James." I opened it and, to my horror, it itemized word for word how he was going to die and then be honored. Lilac was named. I went into the living room for a few minutes and screamed into the pillow until my throat was so raw I had to take some cough drops.

"So what now? Where do we take this from here?" Rose asked.

"We e-mail the President the NP video and cc all the news outlets," I said.

"There's no way that's going to make the news or anything legitimate," she replied.

"Don't be so sure. Normally I'd agree with you, but we're talking about the Solex family here. Also, we're going to blind cc the foreign press," I said.

"Why don't we just blind cc everybody?" she asked

"That would be the smart thing to do. E-mail her and blind cc everyone else. But, no. I want the President to think I'm directing traffic toward the press. That I think I can just e-mail them and get one over on her. I want her to think that I'm stupid. I want to draw her out. I'm going to get her to admit to everything. This ends soon," I finished.

"You okay, hon?" Rose said.

"Just send the thing out," I replied.

Sure enough, within ninety minutes of sending the e-mail, Blur Slanders was interrupting his own yarbling yamhole with breaking news. Streaming footage from Saturnalian Watermark with Jean being lead out in handcuffs. Not a moment later, an e-mail reply from the President's secretary telling me how infuriated she was with me for the way I went about this and that she was coming to Mass to deal with this after she'd dealt with a few internal things. I was thinking that deep down she must have known I hadn't played all my cards yet and maybe had something showing that her hands were dirty. Otherwise, why wouldn't she just send someone to kill us instead of coming to meet us? Maybe she thought she could negotiate with money? Maybe bring people to muscle the rest of our info out of us and get all copies of it? Who knows. Either way, we were going to meet. She said no phones or digital cameras and not to try anything funny because she could detain me as an enemy combatant if she so chose for "leaking sensitive information of a national security interest." No way I was going without Rosette and Hannah. Thinking back once more to French-kissing that skeleton. I needed to make sure I had every angle covered. I looked over at James's letter. There were only a few lines left that hadn't been decoded. I sat down and closed my eyes for a minute and took a deep breath. Nothing in this world is an accident. I could really use your help, NP, I thought.

Suddenly I had this explosion of colors like a

kaleidoscope shattering deep in my mind, color crystals just falling everywhere. I felt like I was on a roller coaster from my mind into outer space, but it was like a bungee cord. I could see it. It was a shiny gray one. When I got to the farthest pull of the cord I reached my hand out and plucked this enormous book out of thin air that had all the information I could ever want or ask for in the world. I read a huge section of it. During this time, I felt this absolute feeling of warmth and comfort. Just as fast as I shot out, the bungee cord started pulling me back. I dropped the book and flew back through the layers of the stratosphere and the atmosphere and collapsed back into my mind. It felt like diving into a pool. I felt a jolt. In an instant, I forgot everything I had read. I can't explain it but this profoundly changed my life. I opened my eyes, looked at the paper and the board. I've got this, I thought.

"Hannah, I need you to use my Shui to figure out how Atlantis disappeared," I said, looking back to James's Atlantis reference in his letter.

I e-mailed the President back with the scrambler, of course telling her I wasn't in the area and asking her if she liked my first e-mail, but that I would be back soon. We could meet then.

"I'll be right back," I said

"Where are you going?" Hannah asked.

"I've got an idea."

With that, I went into Jean's room where he kept a tin box under his bed with about $25,000 inside. Well, he'd be in jail for at least ten to fifteen years. I mean, even for a lawyer of his family's caliber, it's hard to argue video evidence of a forced suicide. Even dressed up as an excited college grad in graduation regalia and waving a gun like a bad B-movie actor, an insanity plea would still land him in the puzzle box for years, during which time they would fill him up with plenty of meds. Thing is, in this world, you may have money, but nobody wants to hire the crazy guy. He might as well own up to it and do the hard time in pound-me-in-the-ass prison. Because I knew when he got out, at least he might have an option. Actually, that is not a decision I wanted to ever face. Just like Rosibuild, he could donate to the cause. I threw on a pair of sunglasses, a hat, and a hoodie in case my building was being watched, and went out the back fire escape. This must be what celebrities feel like. The free sex is definitely not worth it. You know what? I forgot one thing. Went back inside the house and went to all the hiding spots, grabbed every bottle of alcohol in the house and put it in a bag, then took it out the window.

"Excuse me, sir! Who the hell are you and what did you do to my friend?" Rose said.

"I can't believe what I'm seeing," Hannah added.

I dumped the bag in the trash and took off down the alleyway. The SeaMart was just down the block.

CHAPTER 19

This entire chain of events had been a test of her patience and she couldn't stop thinking about how she couldn't wait until she was able to put it behind her. Unfortunately for Lilac, she didn't have all the pieces to the puzzle yet, and without them she would not be able to move forward with anything. As stupid as it sounded, this was one of the biggest tests of her presidency; this whole nonsense that James Newsdon had caused. What the hell did he do in Amsterdam and why was it that her people couldn't get any answers for her?

"I want a full status report on James in Amsterdam, as well as what his brother has been up to in Boston," Lilac fumed to Roger.

"Right away, Madam President," Roger replied.

God, this was annoying. She had an easier time getting intelligence on the Ivory Coast or North Africa than she did on this one clearly troubled kid and his escapades in Europe.

"Madam President, I'm sorry but our trail goes cold after we caught him checking out at the Swissotel. We have absolutely nothing until he re-enters Germany," Roger replied.

"Goddammit, Roger, that's not good enough," Lilac said. It blew her mind that with all the advantages they had at their disposal, this kid just disappeared off the grid. She was so sure that he was up to something, even if most of those closest to her had told her to drop this a while ago. It reminded her of the time that she was campaigning and her advisors told her that the Water Protection Act commercials were dangerous to her campaign as President, even as she insisted that she had to see them through. Turned out she rode those commercials all the way into the White House. She was right about that, so why couldn't they just trust her that something serious was going on here? She fully felt that she had earned her stripes over and over again and yet somehow she kept having to push the crowd forward on this investigation. Nothing infuriated her more than having to explain herself time and time again. The truth was that she had some deep and dark secrets that she wasn't proud from in her first term, some of which included the overseas Syria action that James was a part of. She didn't know what he knew or what he didn't know but the truth was that it was irrelevant. He was an obstacle, in her way, at this point even in death, and she had to make sure nothing fishy had happened.

"Lilly, if you need my help, you're going to have to tell me what's going on here. I can't keep operating under the assumption that you have been completely honest with me," Jake came out with. The truth was that Jake had felt that there were certain aspects of this wild-goose chase that went above his head. That he was missing pieces to. That he was not being filled in completely on briefings, and that hurt him deeply. He had been nothing but loyal and went above the call of duty to make sure everything in the President's life was copasetic and comfortable for her. If she couldn't trust him, then who could she trust? "Lilly, we've always been close. Just talk to me. Tell me exactly what's going on here," Jake pleaded.

"Meet me in the Lincoln Room in fifteen," Lilac said. She hated that room, but she was at the point now where she needed some help.

"You got it, Lilly," Jake replied.

Lilac spent the next ten minutes pacing up and down past the door, puffing on her fake cigarette and chewing Nicorette. The thought crossed her mind that as long as she wasn't smoking and taking in all those toxins, she might be able to ride the fake cigarette and gum train to her grave. It's not like she was breaking a promise to her husband. Unfortunately, this was not helping the ball of nerves jonesing in the pit of her stomach since Jake had spoken to her. Maybe this was a good thing, her being able to let loose and explain herself to someone. She had been keeping such secrets from those closest to her; this might be a cathartic and, who knows, maybe even helpful.

"Lilly, how are you? God, you look like hell. What's been going on with you lately? I feel like you're in your own little world. You're stuck, focused on this dead Marine, and I just have no idea what happened to my friend," Jake said.

"Oh, you know, business as usual," Lilac replied.

"Lilly, why don't you cut the crap and tell me what's really up with you."

"Jake, can you take a seat for me," Lilac said.

"All right, but you have to tell me what's going on because I can't help you if you don't talk to me," he replied.

"Oh, it's so complicated, Jake," Lilly said as she puffed on her fake cigarette. "The truth is that I don't know where to begin."

"Why don't you just tell me what's been going on with you lately. You don't seem like yourself and it's getting harder for me to explain to the Joint Chiefs of Staff why you've been so off. You've got to give me something, Lilly."

"This is so hard for me to tell you. I know you have always been there for me, but this time I might have really fucked up."

"What are you talking about?" Jake said.

"The situation with the Newsdon kid is not as simple as you've been led to believe. God, I don't know where to start with this."

"Lilly, you know you can tell me anything.

We've been together through so much. Through your first two terms as senator. I've been around for a while, and I promise you that nothing you tell me today will jeopardize our relationship. But you have to be honest with me. I can't help you if you keep beating around the bush," Jake finished.

"All right," Lilac said. "This is difficult for me to say, but just understand that I had no choice in the matter." Lilac took a deep breath. "James Newsdon was part of a clandestine mission on the border of Syria to help take out the leader of the insurgents. They were in south Damascus, doing routine missions, nothing special initially, until they got attacked by a convoy of locals and barely survived it. It was our idea to pull them out. We sent them to Ankara in Turkey to hold for further instructions. While there, it was documented that James had spoken out against the mission in Syria and because of him, two people defected and pretty much disappeared off the map. He became very vocal against the mission they were sent there for. But it was deeper than that," Lilac said as she took a deep breath from her e-cigarette. "James was part of a covert mission of programmed assassins."

"Wait, what do you mean programmed?" Jake asked.

"I mean trained," Lilac said as she wondered if she'd slipped.

"I see," Jake said. "So what I don't understand

is what this kid did that makes you see him as such a liability."

"He knew things with this mission that could jeopardize our play in the region. He had surveillance of underground bunkers and weapons stockpiles. He knew the names of all the key players in the area. His mission was to covertly take them out. But something went wrong and they were found out. They barely survived the onslaught. It was from that point that things went a little off with his group. They started missing checkpoints and communications with us. We had to send in an extraction group to get them out of there. When they got to Turkey, things changed. We didn't have our super soldiers anymore. They were broken. Suffering from PTSD. They were a liability at this point due to what they knew. We knew that the mission was over or at the very least that we had to start over with a new team. All the time spent and money and resources we put into training them and getting them in place were lost and we knew that we probably wouldn't be able to duplicate our initial plan. So we had to reprogram them," Lilac finished.

"Reprogram them; what's that mean, exactly?" Jake replied.

"We had to clean their slates. Start from scratch. Implant new memories. It was our only shot at salvaging what abilities they had left. Except something went terribly wrong."

"What exactly would that be?" Jake asked nervously.

"It made James worse. It was like poking an angry dog with a stick. After the initial round of conditioning, James kept talking about how he was going to tell everyone at home what went on overseas and reach out to former Marines to get their testimonies as well. He quickly deteriorated after a few weeks and then one day he just shot himself. Point blank."

"Jesus. But it was a clean suicide, right?" Jake asked.

"Well, not exactly. A few people in his group found out what happened and became inconsolable. It was the straw that broke the camel's back. They became rowdy, scared, angry—all the above, I imagine. They were dangerous loaded weapons. So it became clear that something had to be done." Lilac paused. She took a drag of her fake cigarette and waited for this information to sink in.

"God, Lilly, what happened?"

She took a minute to collect her thoughts. She wasn't exactly sure how she was going to explain this next part. "Well, they were working on a checkpoint when we got word that an IED took out their vehicle. Now all the details surrounding it were sketchy, but from the best we could figure out, this was done internally by one of them. By a broken mind that couldn't take it anymore. You were on vacation when this happened. When we got ourselves together, we decided that the best thing to do was say that their mission in Syria was sabotaged and that they had died there. However, James had already made a ton of noise regarding what he was planning on doing; it was hard to keep a lid on him, so we decided that telling people he saved the survivors and was a hero was cleaner than having to explain to everyone that he had killed himself earlier. Technically it was true. We knew the public outrage that would result if they found out that an entire convoy went off the map mentally. This took a lot of maneuvering and cost us a ton of money, but it worked," Lilac finished.

"That must have been such a hard decision to make, Lilly. I had no idea just how deep this goes. I understand why you think he might have been up to something. I'll help; just tell me what you need from me," Jake replied.

As Lilac poured herself a glass of wine, she turned to Jake and smiled. She was so happy she had someone close to her who she could talk with. Unfortunately, she wasn't telling the entire truth. Truth was that she had flown over to Ankara and had met with all of them. She'd met with James shortly before he killed himself. The content of their meeting needed to be kept secret from everyone because it was the one secret that could cause the greatest controversy since Watergate.

CHAPTER 20

"So, what did you get?" Hannah asked as I climbed back in the window.

"This." I dropped a bag of forty flash drives on the table.

"Run out of space to store your porn?" Rose quipped. "I mean, we do have Rosibuild's drive now. This was an unnecessary war chest expenditure that could have been appropriated as front-row tickets for The Rising," Rosette added.

"What did you find while I was gone?" I asked.

"You got these at SeaMart? Why didn't you go to the store down the road?" Hannah asked.

"I just e-mailed the President from a scrambler with stolen information from an undercover voyeur Jesuit murderer. The last thing I want to do is show my face in a techie store that is overloaded with recording devices so they can track what I'm about to do," I said.

While they talked, I started copying all the files from the hard drive onto the flash drives and memory cards. It's amazing how big the first storage drive was in the 1960s and how it held nothing compared to what they can hold now. I also started putting envelopes together to send to the news, both traditional and alternative. I also sent this out to the people NP felt were the real international movers and shakers, who could make a real difference in the world with this kind of information and who could blow the lid off this whole operation. Everything was laid out ready, dead to rights.

I also found a file called "WAPA." I remember having a ton of arguments with NP regarding the WAPA Act that was shot down a few years back by the President. WAPA stood for the Water Privatization Act of 2018. Long story short, a bunch of companies thought it would be a profitable and bright idea to privatize water and she "bravely" stood up against it, gathering a coalition that shot the act down. There were a ton of obligatory politically motivated commercials such as her pouring water out of a pitcher with orange slices for poor children in Florida. NP thought she was just campaigning in a swing state. Anyway, this act was shut down and she was viewed as this hero and it propelled her to the White House. I'll never forget her stupid slogan after it was all done. "We came, we saw, you dried up."

"What do you have for me?" I asked.

"You wanted to know about Atlantis…well, you've heard of Edgar Cayce, right?" Hannah quizzed.

"Yeah. NP used to talk about him like crazy. Said he was able to access something or other to gain his information. Was like Nostradamus, only looked like your grandfather and slept a lot," I joked.

"You're an ass. Do you know what he wrote about Atlantis?" Hannah asked.

I froze. This was what I had been waiting for since the "experience" I'd just had. "Go on."

"Well, you should have. According to him, the Atlanteans built giant crystal power plants. Crystals were used for any and everything regarding power sources. Atlantis sank into the ocean as Plato wrote in *Timaeus* and *Critias*: 'In a single day and night of misfortune.' Okay, so, this was the first mention of Atlantis. However, according to Cayce, it was through the overcharging of the crystal that it exploded."

"Fascinating," I said.

"All the New Agers believe in them and their powers and energy. Then she stopped for a second time and looked at me and noticed the face I was wearing. Do you know what chronological ethnocentrism is?" she asked.

"Isn't it when we consistently wipe out races?" I replied jokingly.

"Close, foolio. It's the collective mindset that because we're the latest generation alive, we are the furthest along technologically, socially, medicinally, spiritually. Basically, we are the smartest and they were stupid. You get my drift.

We look at anyone in the past like they were in the Flintstone age," Hannah finished.

"BAM BAM!" Rosette added.

"Exactly. Now look at this." Hannah showed me this article she found about how scientists were able to use lasers to store information on crystals. The technology was very young of course but...*holy shit!* I tripped over myself a few times. Have you ever seen a cat cut a corner and Tokyo drift after you've just mopped the floor and it can't catch its footing? I'm lucky I didn't tear my ACL. I grabbed my brother's things, throwing the perfectly folded American flag on the couch and grabbed his necklace that I now recognized as a crystal and not just some dumb rock. I looked at it and with my hands trembling, I looked at his letter. "Do you think that means long after I'm gone that you can look up to the sky, in those crystals, and see a part of me?" and "How we fell off Atlantis," "So many blind anger, can only be cured by learning." People will keep fighting on this planet until they are made aware of the truth. I looked back online. This technology was so young. Well, maybe it wasn't at one point but it was then. The company Senna Ore Inc. that specialized in crystal embedding had a small US branch in Rhode Island, my Internet searching would lead me to understand. Took a little while for me to find it; it seemed like they almost didn't want to be found. Well, that wasn't too far from us.

Headquartered in Amsterdam. So, is that why James went to Amsterdam and blew all his money on this crazy science? To embed a secret that nobody could figure out? The watch, I mean, that's one thing but this, a whole other ballgame. Let's just hope we weren't wrong. Well, I mean it's the only lead we had at that point and the clock was ticking on the visit from the President.

"Rose, love, need you to do me one more favor," I said.

"Anything. What's up?" she said.

"You said one of your swim friends was heading back home for the weekend and lives in Rhode Island? See if she wants a ride."

"Why?"

"Need her to bring this in to a post office and have them stamped."

"Out of state…not one of our faces…got it," she replied.

"I don't want any of us near a camera for this. They won't think twice if it's a local res," I said.

"I just said that," she retorted.

"Just make the call. Pack a bag, too," I said as I headed in to pack my own overnight bag alongside Hannah.

As her friend got ready while we headed over there, I kept thinking back to what NP had said about 1s and 0s and holographic information. It sounds crazy, but then you look at a crystal or a phone and realize the data that is stored in them, that life, is more like a surreal videogame than anything else. My mind had been reset more times than I could count. Reality was the only drink I needed anymore. I had been given the best gift from two who were no longer with me. My mind had opened up to the endless possibilities of potential. I couldn't wrap my brain around why others would want to hurt and take away this feeling of boundless knowledge and love and trap them in mental paradigms that make no sense once you'd begun to decode the Phoenix. I immediately connected with a quote I'd heard from a comedian my brother used to watch. I was very young and he died I think before I was even born. My brother had tapes of him. "The world is like a ride in an amusement park. And when you choose to go on it, you think it's real because that's how powerful our minds are. And the ride goes up and down and round and round. It has thrills and chills and it's very brightly colored and it's very loud and its fun, for a while. Some people have been on the ride for a long time and they begin to question: 'Is this real, or is this just a ride?' And other people have remembered, and they come back to us, they say, "Hey, don't worry, don't be afraid, ever, because this is just a ride." And we kill those people."

CHAPTER 21

We were halfway to Newport. Man, time flies when you have a mission.

"So, we were talking about the morning star, aka Lucifer, aka Venus, a while back, right? It was also a name for the Virgin Mary Morning Star that is, or—wow, shit—didn't realize, the Virgo Mary. Virgin Mary in the Litany of Loreto," said Hannah as she periodically looked up from the tablet.

"What is that exactly?" I asked.

"Well, it says here that it was originally approved by Pope Sixtus the Fifth. Look right here: Ark of the Covenant, Gate of Heaven, MORNING STAR."

"Why do you bring that up?" Rose asked.

"I just find it interesting. Look, it says here that, 'The Dominicans, at their general chapter held at Bologna in 1615, ordered it to be recited in all the convents of their order after the Office on Saturdays, at the end of the customary Salve Regina," she said.

"What's the point?" I jumped in.

"I just find it interesting that we're going to Newport where Salve Regina University is. Just making connections is all," Hannah replied.

"Good stuff, Husker. This is Noah, by the way" Rose added.

"Hey all," Noah replied. Noah for a girl's name? I'm not so sure.

"Ooh, I love it for a girl's name," Hannah said. Of course she did.

"Thanks. Me too. When you're young, you tend to be self-conscious about being different but as you get older you like it. It's funny. You spend the first twenty years of your life wanting to fit in and the rest of it wanting to stand out," she replied. Girl had some wisdom. NP used to say that as an individual you spend the first twenty-five years of your life cultivating your ego and if you've evolved properly, the rest of your life trying to obliterate it.

"You do know what you need to do for us, right?" I asked. I had to make sure.

"Yeah, it's fine. Just drop me off at the post office. I'm meeting some peeps downtown by the boats anyway. You just need them stamped, right?" Noah asked.

"Exactly," I said.

We bullshat around for the last forty-five minutes. We dropped her off a block away from the post office. Ten minutes later she was out, walking down the street, chucking up the deuces and blowing kisses. We sped off in search of Senna Ore. As a precautionary measure, we were using handwritten directions, no GPS, so they couldn't satellite track. We all turned our phones off. An out-of-state drive would be a red flag to those closest to me at this point in the game. Plus, I had two of my friends abroad, one in England and one in Hong Kong, sign onto my e-mail and send dummy e-mails inquiring about contacts for their local news organizations immediately after I received the President's e-mail. It would confuse them. Wild card. Secondly, when they read the e-mail, they would spend time wasting away on these two countries and it should give us the time we needed to put our end game together. After circling for what seemed like an hour, we found the place. We actually saw it a few times but it was just so unassuming we kept driving past it. We were greeted by a man whistling at the front door.

"Hello, all. I'm Conrad Helmharn. I'm the expert in extracting information who you spoke to. Very few know of our existence. I'm interested. What exactly do you need from me?"

"Is there any way we can do this like the oldest profession in the world? We give you money, you take care of our needs, no questions asked, and then pretend we were never here? Maybe let us cry a little bit at the end?" I snidely replied. I'd just assumed if we found him, he would know exactly what we needed of him.

"We don't exactly work like that, but please come inside," he said.

He led us in through his building. I have to

admit, book by its cover. From the outside, you wouldn't have given it a second thought but from the inside you would have thought they'd buried King Tut there. It was large, decadent. There was ambience like I've never felt before and I had done holidays with the Solex family a few times. We're talking *Eyes Wide Shut*-type galas. I guess it's not the size but what you do with it. Damnit! Don't read into that. Helmharn walked to the middle of the room, hands folded behind his back, turned to us, looked at each of us for a few minutes, then calmly spoke:

"I see you taking in the decor of this place, although I must say that money is not everything in the world. You will come to learn that. I was watching this comedian the other day and he said money can't buy you happiness; it only makes you more of what you already are. So if you are an alcoholic and you're broke, when you're down to your last five dollars it's last call. But what if you were a millionaire? Alas, in this world, there are only two types of truth tellers left and you won't find them on the news: comedians and novelists. They can both hide under the disguise of jokes, premises, and in the land of make-believe while burying truth. You just have to be smart enough and want it enough to take the time to find the message. Anybody who walks through these doors has to have an incredible level of outside-the-box thinking to even recognize the possibility of what I, what we, do here. For that, I say the original price I told you, cut it in half, but you must tell me what you came here for," he finished.

Only $10,000 now. Money wasn't everything, he was right, but money wasn't my concern at this point in the game.

"I don't give a shit about the money. The last time I told someone, my best friend ended up being sacrificed. Not killed. I mean a taped ritual. How can I trust you? Who are you really?" I honestly have no idea where that came from.

"Interesting. Your secret is above the money. You obviously understand the point I was just making. I can't tell you how happy that makes me, Mr. Newsdon."

Wait, what? How the hell did this guy know who I am?

"I know exactly who you are, Mr. Newsdon, I recognized you the moment I heard your voice and again when I saw you exiting your vehicle outside. I saw you on TV at your brother's funeral. I am so sorry for your loss. I can only imagine this is related to his overseas handling. He paid cash at our Amsterdam location to embed some information. I'm assuming you have it. Good. You can keep this as a necklace when you're done; it won't harm it at all. Let me reintroduce myself. My name is Conrad Helmharn-Solex. I'm Jean's second cousin. When

I saw the story on the news, my heart sank. Some of them, they make a sacrifice to rise in the ranks. I'm ashamed to be related. I would do this for you for free, Mr. Newsdon, and my most humble apologies for what a pig I have in my family, but I have to keep this store running, you understand. Eight-thousand," he said.

"Thank you. How long will this take?" I asked, eager to get this underway. Would they slice the crystal into small filings then put it in a box like Einstein's brain? Would they burn it? Crystal technology is not something I am familiar with.

"Let me just check our internal system. Oh, it looks like it was only two files. Not long at all and you can watch if you'd like. You will all need to wear these goggles, though. Unless you want to be a Mr. Magoo."

We watched as Mr. Helmharn-Solex guided a laser as it changed colors. Once it got to jungle green, he controlled it like a joystick in a pilot game and brought it over the crystal. He locked into it and clicked a button which then opened the point beam into a square and held it over the crystal for roughly thirty seconds until we saw the joystick and crystal jolt slightly. He then guided the laser to a glass plate. "This part takes a little longer. A crystal has infinitely more space than glass or silicon. They're the future of hard drives. Hopefully I will live to see them realized, but doubtful." He smiled.

After a few minutes, the joystick shook again; the glass plate had holders in place to make sure it didn't shake and shatter. He turned the laser off and then slid the glass plate into the computer and two flash drives into the USB ports.

"Why two flash drives?" I asked.

"Why do they implant two embryos when you get in vitro?" he asked.

"Enlighten me. I don't have a vagina," I retorted.

"It's so you get your money's worth. Doubles the chances of successful results!" he explained.

After a few minutes, the glass disk popped out and the flash drives were done. Quick ten-minute process. The future of intelligence gathering. Or homework and porn trading. I dunno. I can't see a hundred years into the future; can you? I took one of them and put it into the Mizo as my tablet had died right before we got here. There was a password, though. Not good.

"Uh, excuse me, but there is a password on here," I quipped.

"I copied it exactly as it was saved on their end. This isn't security on our end. Your brother did this. Je suis desole, mon ami," he said as he walked toward an office in the corner.

Clue: They try to teach us in church that the answer is in what sustains us, but what they don't teach us is that in this new age, the answer is in what sustains us.

Shit, the last part of the letter that went unsolved.

"It's Jesus, right? Try it," Rosette said.

Tried it. The screen shook and said incorrect. Three more tries. Damn it, there was a counter on this, too?

"Maybe it's caps sensitive. Try J-esus," Hannah added.

Tried it and the screen shook. Clue: The password is not caps sensitive.

Thanks, asshole. Two tries left.

"Air?" Rose gulped.

"Huh?" I said.

"You'd be dead without it, right?" Rose said.

Good one. Tried it. Screen shook. Damn it! Last try. Not sure what was going to happen next. Not sure if I could use the other flash drive or if I was completely screwed. I had to think.

"I'll be right back," I said as I escaped for some air.

I went outside. It was evening and the wind off the water went right up my nose, into my brain, where it landed on my hippocampus and brought back Polaroid synapses of Hannah and I coming here. Each year we'd summer for a week or two, walk down the pier, rent scooters, and maybe take a boat ride. It's funny because things were so quiet then and in a way those were the better days. We would stay at this same little bed-and-breakfast a few blocks from the main road. Sometimes we would drive down around the mansions that were built for the wealthiest of the wealthy, but which have now been preserved by the community. We'd walk down the overlook where you could climb down and walk out onto the piles of rocks that stab out into the sea like Triton's pitchfork. This is where I fell in love with her and knew I was going to be with her for the rest of my life. I had buried my head up my ass so long with the idea that life would start after I was a doctor that I'd almost missed being able to live in the moment from twenty-five to thirty. Thankfully I had a best friend who reminded me of that before he died. God, this clean, fresh water was seriously unlike anything I'd...

"Rose!" I ran back in with an epiphany.

"Yeah, babe."

"They try to teach us in church that the answer is in what sustains us. Jesus or, more specifically, the messages of Jesus. The book weaves through life and symbolism; it's a gorgeous symbiosis of love that we all need to just focus on instead of those trying to harm others. The golden rule: live humbly; his parables are those to live by and make yourself better by. I mean, who wouldn't want to live by those messages? It's the rest of it; it just got so twisted with..." I was cut off.

"Where are you going with this?" Rose replied.

"What they don't teach us is that in this new age, the answer is in what sustains us. You were on the right track, but it's not air. It's water. New age: Aquarius," I triumphed. I typed in water and a picture of my brother giving me a thumbs-up came up on the screen, then him riding a broom and spanking his ass while he swept away the password screen. Thanks, James. Helmharn-Solex was right. There were two files. One was a video; the other was a document. I opened the document with butterflies for what the video could possibly show. The adrenaline shits building in my stomach were terraforming in different dimensions.

The document was a file from a university that pioneered a way to use solar energy to take water, separate the hydrogen and oxygen molecular bond, then use the hydrogen as clean fuel. This would eliminate the need for fossil fuel. My mind started racing. I remembered reading about Tesla and how he developed a way to give electricity to the world, but was shut down and at the end of his life ended up broke and in love with a bird. I remembered the quote from that physicist he put in his first writing, talking about how life on other planets is searched for by the top scientists. Well, additional life on other planets. Type-One civilization harnessed the planetary power. Weather control. I remember hearing a few Olympics ago that China practiced cloud seeding to make sure it didn't rain during the opening and closing ceremonies. That it is possible to blow clouds away and that it is also possible to make it rain. Some say that earthquake manipulation is possible with floor-level tectonic-plate manipulation. It seems to me that we've mastered Type One and were on our way to Type Two This would be getting energy directly from the mother star. Using the power of the sun to energize the machines. *That* would be where this would be taking us! I got incredibly excited, which was immediately followed by a knot in my stomach.

All at once, I began to understand why my brother had to go. He had broken down the control of the world through the Bible and had stumbled across the clean-fuel solution. These both have unbelievable consequences in the Middle East. This would have put not only the giant oil companies out of business, but would have also severely changed the politics of the world. Imagine, if oil was insignificant, what that would do to the Middle East, the banking structure. Always follow the money trail. For a few extra dollars, I was able to use Helmharn-Solex's printer. I printed one copy for everyone, then sat for a moment and printed another one.

"G. You're going to want to come see this," Hannah said. Crap. Hannah only called me G. when there was a serious situation. I rushed back over. They started it back at the beginning.

It looked like a video angle from the hip. Damn it; it must be the watch camera. Then I heard my brother's voice.

"Sarge just left. You know that feeling I was telling you about? The one when you're on the pirate ship and it's all the way up and starting to drop and you and your balls feel weightless? I'm starting to feel it again and this is usually the point where it gets fuzzy, so I'm starting this recorder to see what goes on."

The next five minutes are mundane, just James doing a bunch of push-ups, sit-ups, and reading. Then he starts walking down the hallway and enters a room with two-sided glass and a projection screen on the other side. The room is dark; you can't make out the faces around the horseshoe table, but on the project screen is a very familiar face. Lilac Northinly.

"¿Que tal Santiago?"

Wait, what the hell was I seeing?

"Estoy bien, mi amor!" James said.

"That's good, Santiago. That's very good. Lo siento, senor. It looks like James survived yesterday. He's a lot tougher than we expected. I didn't want to have to call on you, but the day we talked about, that last-case scenario, the one we tried to put off, has unfortunately come up. James has been incredibly difficult with us and the mission. We've tried to reason with him but he just won't work with us. We need you to take him out. ¿Crees que puedes hacerlo?" the President said.

Was she seriously talking to my brother in the fourth person?

"YO haría lo que fuera para usted mi reina!" he replied in perfect Spanish.

"Good. Give it a month. It'll give his brother time to grieve over the holiday. Make it the 21st. It'll be around Thanksgiving then. It'll take a few days for us to bring him back to the States, you understand."

"Entiendo completamente."

The screen shut off, closing around her evil smirk. The watch cut off. He must have seen the video he recorded and knew his time was limited and there was nothing he could do about it. Knowing how much time he had left, he must have looked this company up and flew to Amsterdam with his savings. A dying man's secret, entrusting his brother, who was completely asleep, to figure it out. His alternative personality was going to kill him, not realizing they were one and the same. The power of the moment overwhelmed me. He didn't have PTSD; he wasn't a loose cannon. I needed air again. I walked outside from where we were, and then continued walking. I kept walking all the way to the Hyatt on Goat Island, about a mile and a half away. I wasn't sure where I was going but when I saw the lighthouse I just followed it. Looked up and saw

Orion's Belt. Maybe we really do need to rethink our chronological ethnocentrism. Rosette drove alongside me the entire time at two miles an hour, not saying a word. It was nighttime at this point. I rented the biggest suite. Goat Island. How fitting. Capricorn and, wouldn't you know, this was my mental rebirth from the ashes. I just began the monster climb up the mountain that would take the President down. This ends tomorrow, I thought.

CHAPTER 22

"What the fuck!" Lilac shrieked. "I *knew* there was something more to James; I knew it. Didn't I tell you?" Lilac ferociously asked Roger.

"Okay, we need to calm down. We can spin this," Jake replied from the back of the room.

"How exactly is that going to be possible? They went to the press already. Now everybody on TV is calling for the head of whomever set that up. We're going to be finished here."

"Not necessarily," Jake replied. "You didn't have anything directly to do with this. We can spin this to make it look like those two acted on their own."

"They're going to be able to trace our phone call to him. Bank accounts, everything," Lilac said.

"No they're not. We called him from a prepaid cell phone and none of those bank accounts can be traced back to anyone. You didn't think we had this angle covered?" Roger replied.

Lilac couldn't handle much more stress. She had already gone through her pack of electronic cigarettes that were supposed to last her a week in only three days. "I want to go see these kids. I want to do it quickly and discreetly," she said.

"Madam President, are you sure that's such a good idea right now? I mean, it'll be a little hard for us to clear your schedule; plus, what exactly do you hope to accomplish?"

"I have no idea, but I need to put an end to this. I can't risk any more information coming out. I don't even know what additional information they have right now, and that's seriously pissing me off," Lilac replied.

"Let's just take a deep breath and think about this for a minute."

"No. There's nothing to think about. We're going to Boston. Call that little bastard Graham and tell him we're coming. Roger, clear my schedule. Tell them I'm sick and need a day. If anything is truly important, put the documents together and bring them on the flight."

As Jake began to make the calls to clear her schedule, he wondered what else there could be that had the President all bent out of shape. If the story of what really happened to James would come out in the news, then they could spin it, make it seem like he went rogue. Unfortunately, it happens all the time. Maybe Lilly did have a good heart by trying to keep the truth away from the American public; he just didn't want to see her be taken down because of it. Little did he know she had a much greater involvement in this than she let on.

CHAPTER 23

Girls were up by eight and we were out by nine. I had been up for two hours already going over everything in my head so as not to make any mistakes. I didn't want to be some skeleton that some vice president had to dance with on inauguration night in the basement of the White House, like at my fraternity.

"We just have to swing by a mailbox on the way back. Just need to borrow your Mizu one more time," I said to Rose.

Plugged in the scrambler once more and went on Skype. Made the phone call to the White House.

"WZ #1526. Where? Who? Who is with her? I just want to know. Well, then where does she want to meet? Hancock Cemetery? Is this a joke? What is this, *The Godfather*? No, I'm not going to meet there. Call me superstitious. Because it doesn't sound like a healthy decision. Are you high? Okay, then are you a temp? Hold on a second." I saw a mailbox in front of a florist across the street as we were stopped at a red light. "Stop the car, Rose—stop the car. Is your name Rose, lady? Then why are you answering?

Listen, I am not meeting there. You can tell her to meet us at the park behind the Masons' lodge in Braintree in two hours if she's already in town." I hung up.

I jumped out to dump an envelope into a mailbox. A flash drive with a sticky note and password of all my brother's writings, NP's writings, and the information from the crystal to the Zip Code Bandits.

CHAPTER 24

"I hate coming to this town; it's always so cold," Lilac said.

"Do you want me to turn the heat up in the car? Alex said. Lilac had managed to clear her schedule and bring her two most eager bodyguards, Alex and Steve, along for the trip. It was mostly for her protection. Even when she dressed down, there would be people that recognized her. She wasn't exactly in great graces with most of the country at that point.

"No, it's fine. How long until we get there?" Lilac asked.

"GPS says twenty minutes. Are we sure we're going to meet them at a park?" Steve asked.

"It'll be fine. It's a big public park. We'll be able to have our privacy. However, if something goes wrong, I need to be able to get the hell out of there, you understand?"

"Yes ma'am," they replied simultaneously.

Lilac kept going over everything in her head that had happened. She knew there were plenty of things she had done that she wasn't proud of, but everything she did she thought she was doing for the greater good. It wasn't her fault that things had gotten so messy. Why didn't those damn kids come to her first before going to the news? This was just going to make her life more difficult. Still, she had a strange feeling that this wasn't going to be over once they left Boston.

CHAPTER 25

We weren't back in town ten minutes when an unmarked car pulled up and the President stepped out with these two massive men. I handed her the flowers and winked at her. She looked at me, disgusted.

"You've got balls, kid. You're an idiot, but have a set. I know if I had a pair like yours swinging between my legs instead of this string, people would take me much more seriously. Like when I say to call me if they have any more information, I mean just that and not run to the press. You know that these two Secret Service agents will put a bullet in your head if you even fart in my general direction." She drew the first line.

"You can't kill an idea, lady," I replied, sizing her up.

"Ha. The drunken med student is a revolutionary now? Please."

I pulled my hand out of my coat pocket. I had five panic 130db key chains, one on each finger. "What kind of echo and resonance do you think this would carry? Where did you tell your staff you are? Where does Washington think you are right now? What if an entire town saw you here? Most of them don't know what a diabolical psycho you really are; they'd probably just mob you for autographs and pictures. I've got the head of the Zip Code Bandits on speed dial just dying for a story. Also, I've got a scope trained on your car and your men right now." I continued: "Apparently leaving two men alive out of James's team wasn't the smart thing to do. Say hi, guys."

I may have forgotten to mention this. During my brother's funeral, I had exchanged phone numbers with the two Marines from his platoon. They were both surprisingly local, only a few hours in either direction. I had reached out to them the day before on my walk to Goat Island and sent them the video of James and the President. They made their way up and set up shop immediately. I had planned the location at which to meet the President all along. I knew she would meet me; I was just confirming they were set up, and right now they were dancing red scopes on the Secret Service agents.

"Professional killers like you programmed, Madam President. Don't bother trying to locate them. They're probably bouncing the laser off preset mirrors," I replied, sensing a turn in the conversation.

"What is it that you want, MacGyver? I have a DoD briefing in the morning and McKayla's not impressed by your silly Team Six. Also, those

Marines will be taken care of."

"Like you took care of 'Santiago'? I asked.

"Excuse me?"

"See, we in the know, know that you're tracing e-mails, monitoring social media, etc. Even tracking transferred files. Even encrypted e-mail programs aren't safe anymore. You can put the rules in place, but we'll always find a way to route around them. You're here because you want to know what I have. Well, here you go. Remember that day you asked me if James sent me any mail? Turns out he did, and then some, but not via post office or e-mail that you could have tracked. This is my brother's watch you returned to me. On it is a letter and a few think pieces for me that break down the entire control of the Western world and its connection with the Vatican." I was readying the kill shot.

"That's a fascinating story," she replied, more than slightly agitated at this point.

"See, this is why I love the truth. Because it has a power that bullshit doesn't. It stands on its own. It doesn't need to capitulate once it's found out." I unscrewed the cap and plugged the watch into the Mizu. The President's eyes opened wide.

"Eventually this led me to the breakdown of the Bible. But my brother didn't stop there. See, he encoded in the message that he knew he was in trouble, so he told me where to find his next message. You got to NP, you got to my brother, but he had a powerful leg up on this situation. He knew what was going to happen to him ahead of time so he could plan for an after-game," I said.

I held up his necklace. The President's eyes went from wide to furious at this point.

"You're a clairvoyant now?" she replied.

"I wonder what the Vatican would do if they knew their catacombs were going to be overrun with people dying to know the truth of their history once this all gets out. How did you get to where you are in this world by being so stupid and closed-minded? I mean, really, it can't just be the same bloodline as the others thing, can it? I'm not even going to bother explaining to you how information can be stored and retracted from these; all you need to know is that he embedded this." And with that I played the video of her talking to James's alternative, Santiago. I have to admit, the sight of the President trying not to urinate on herself was a very empowering feeling. But her being the President, she was an expert at trying to maintain control of a situation.

"What exactly is this supposed to prove?" she said.

"To start? I can prove motive," I said, drawing her in.

"Motive? You are a dumbass, aren't you? The people who make these calls don't answer to courts. Motive? Are you high?" she said as she folded her arms across her chest. Rosette would say in psychology this is a "tell," as people cross over their solar plexus when they feel threatened and in need of protecting themselves. Bingo. Got her.

"You should be very careful with how you word things to me. The other thing on this crystal was the future of Hydrosol. You've been suppressing their research for years to keep the oil business afloat. You can't stop it, though. This is the next step. Power in water. Moving into the Age of Aquarius, Water (Aquarius) being manipulated by its cross sign, Leo's ruling planet, the Sun. That's why my brother had to go. He figured out what you were doing, the why, and how you were doing it. My brother was working to expose this and you had to shut him up. Then my best friend tied it into the Jesuits and their manipulation of people and had to be rubbed out, by a former 'priest' who, from what I can tell, never officially defected and was just planted undercover as a teacher. Except he got himself a wife when he was out, but the order didn't like that very much. You can never have the love of a woman, so they 'made the call.' Then to teach him a lesson, they made him the cameraman the 'Seeing Eye.' Ended up being the eye for my best friend." I paused to let it soak in to the President just how fucked she was. Never underestimate the stubbornness of someone losing control of his or her power.

"Listen, wacko. Even if everything you're saying is true, you've got no proof. Computer technology is amazing. The way you can take a few snips of someone's voice, maybe even from TV, and layer it over some macro-made footage. I can have ten experts attest to this in an hour. I'm the President of the United States, you dumb little shit. Take them in, Alex and Steve. Rough them up a bit before you knock them out. We'll run them through their program when we get back to DC," she finished as the body beef guards approached me.

"Guys, give me a minute before you commit to that because you actually might want to hear what I have to say next, as it involves you. See, I know you're just a puppet, Lilac. D'Israeli said it; Churchill said it; Kennedy said it. Hell, Nixon found out about it and was set up at Watergate over it. You always follow the money. Rule number two. You know what the best part of this all is, though? Guys, you're going to love this. Well, you see, this watch already had the information uploaded to the Mizo. The files I showed you were from the main drive. I set this watch to record. This has been streaming directly to the Zip Code Bandits. I was just showing you how it worked in real time. I'm sure it's on its way to twenty places by now."

"You son of a…" she said before I spoke over her.

"All this information you've just seen, plus

more, is on a combination of flash drives. No e-mails necessary. No way to monitor where it went. No way to block the information from going out. No clue which post office or logistics carrier was used. I told you that we will always route around your new ideas and to watch what you said to me. I do remember giving you a fair chance with that warning. This will all explode onto the scene in no time. It's over. You're over. You took my life, now I'm taking yours. Now agents, you've got two trained snipers on you, I'm sure the Bandits are on their way over here with police and their own news team. If you want, we can switch you two out with my two guys and you can take off. This is your one chance. Again, we're streaming live, remember?" I said.

They actually left. I couldn't believe it. They got in the car and sped off, burning a hole in the grass two-feet deep. They cut the corner just as the Zip Code Bandits were turning with the police. Wouldn't you know who it was?

"Hi, Graham." So now Hitchlords knew my first name. "These guys filled me in on what happened. Wow, I'm going to be on TV. Look, I'm really sorry about before. I've been giving a lot of thought to this and I'd like to take you kids out for a bite to eat when this is all cleared up, to clear the air. Madam President, you have the right to remain silent. Anything you say...." His voice trailed off as I walked back to the girls. We started walking away when one of the Bandits stopped me.

"What's your name?" I asked.

"Pete, um, hey, Mr. Newsdon. I'm sorry about what happened. We loved Mr. Pierce," Pete said.

"Thanks, Peter," I replied.

"But he didn't have half the balls you do. Maybe you should work with us?" he asked. Until that split second, it had never occurred to me to be anything else in this world besides a doctor. That was not the time to decide, but it was an interesting thought.

"Thanks for the offer, Pete. Feel free to stop by anytime. I'd love to hear about the latest work you guys are doing." I smiled.

"Okay, man. You're going to regret that invite. Thanks, buddy. See ya! Quick, get the wide-angle lens. I want to get that sign and the tire marks across from it, as well as the reaction shot. Madam President, smile for the camera," Pete howled.

"Graham? Hey, Graham!" Lilac said.

"Yeah?" I said, turning back to the President.

"You know why my parents named me Lilac? They named me Lilac because it symbolized the turning from winter to spring, the first emotion of love coming into the air. I guess somewhere along the line I forgot that." What was this cheesy, pathetic attempt to buy my good graces? Rosette pushed me out of the way.

"Screw this!" she said. She made a beeline

over to Lilac, cocked back, and decked her in the face.

"Just because you hold people's lives in a business dress doesn't make you any less of a lunatic. That was why my parents named me Rose. It is the flower of love. You took mine from me. Enjoy your time, wherever you end up, when they get their hands on you. Your picture is going to be in the Thesaurus under the words 'fall lady.' Enjoy!"

That was the coolest thing I'd seen in a while. Awesome.

"Can we go home now?" Hannah said.

"Yeah. I'm heading to the pool. I haven't gone swimming in a few days. I feel rusty. I'll catch you guys later, when I'm done processing," Rose said.

"What should we do now, babe?" I asked Hannah as a wave of calm rushed over me that hadn't been there for months.

"Whatever you want, sweetie," she replied.

CHAPTER 26

(SIX MONTHS LATER, AKA NOW)

So now that you're up to speed, here's where we're at. The spinsters behind the scene are slowly basket weaving a story of a renegade downward-spiraling President with a twisted agenda to account for all that's been leaked by my whistle blowing, or should I say flash drive mailing. Throw in a subplot of a grief-ridden former priest who left the clergy for a woman in his congregation, only to lose said wife in a tragic accident which sparks a maniacal obsession with crazy conspiracies and filming sacrifice-type murders and blaming them on the former religious structure he was once a part of. You can't make this up, but is a predictable spin cycle by the media. It's amazing what throngs of people will eat up when they don't want to see the truth of a situation. Rosibuild is currently a candidate for the insanity plea and will definitely wind up in one of the puzzle boxes that they control, and you can be sure they won't rewire his brain to the point that he thinks he's a banana until he dies an old Chiquita. It's okay, though. I didn't expect my story to change the world. Remember the camel to the water story? If you're confused at this point, please place head in toilet and flush. I'm aware that you don't just drop this kind of convoluted think and expect not to have palpable emotions regarding it. I'm actually still waiting for the official public denial from the church and the heresy claim. They're probably doing their research on me, trying to build their discredit campaign strong before they go forth with it. To that, I say two things. Proof is in the pudding, and hopefully people can think on their own. I lost two of the closest and smartest people I've ever loved over this information. Over a BOOK meant for love and some COTTON PAPER. However, that being said, the one thing that I have finally found is a sense of peace and purpose. In spite of everything discussed here, if I could leave you with one message it would be do not let people try to tell you how to be happy or what you need to be happy in your life. Look long and hard at who is telling you what you need and decide if they are leading by example at something you would enjoy emulating. Also, if for some reason I disappear in the future, know that I've quietly taken out life-insurance policies in my name on a few important members of society who are not doing right by us so, if anything should happen to me, just follow the money. You call it paranoia; I call it protection.

Lastly, I want to remind all of you that we

have been a part of something together that nobody else has in the history of human civilization. We have together seen the change of a century, a millennium, and a zodiac sign. Just think about that for a minute. Nobody else can say that but us—this is a truly amazing time. Think about the significance of your life occurring at this very time and what that means for your consciousness. This is the time for a new mental awakening, not to fight about petty misunderstandings or misinterpretations. Love one another and work together to figure our problems out. Most importantly, think for yourselves and do not let anyone tell you what to think. You have a brain that can reason and there is a reason for that. Crap, the light just went on. I have to go. I love you all!

"Welcome back to the new MA Radio, a division of Sibylline Entertainment. Thank you for joining us on this cool summer solstice night. I'm Graham Newsdon, former future doctor and your host. Well, my parents aren't thrilled I dropped out of med school, but there are more important things than money in this world. I'd like to finally deliver a speech that I was going to make at my brother's funeral. Well, it's not mine, it's someone else's, but I'd like to say it all the same: 'War is just a racket. A racket is best described, I believe, as something that is not what it seems to the majority of people. Only a small inside group knows what it is about. It is conducted for the benefit of the very few at the expense of the masses. I believe in adequate defense at the coastline and nothing else. If a nation comes over here to fight, then we'll fight. The trouble with America is that when the dollar only earns six percent over here, then it gets restless and goes overseas to get one-hundred percent. Then the flag follows the dollar and the soldiers follow the flag. I wouldn't go to war again as I have done to protect some lousy investment of the bankers. There are only two things we should fight for. One is the defense of our homes, and the other is the Bill of Rights. War for any other reason is simply a racket.'"

As I finished, Paul, the producer of my show, walked in with a large envelope, waving it frantically at me.

"Here you go, buddy," he said as he walked out of the room, lighting a cigarette on his way.

His hand was shaking and he'd just handed over an envelope with my name typed on it. It was forwarded over from the Zip Code Bandits.

Letter:

It all begins at Christ the Redeemer, all of this. Starting during the age of Leo and coming to a head now. We have the ability to fix something huge and gain wisdom, but you have to tread even lighter because other countries are not going to play as nice as this one does. The key to all wisdom is in the missing capstone to the pyramids.

I spent five minutes re-reading his letter, then a few minutes listening to the tape. At this point, I was fully in because how could you not be? Two things were crystal clear at this point: I was going to need some extra help, and what the hell did I know about Italy?

To Be Continued

96662500R00138

Made in the USA
Columbia, SC
31 May 2018